Copyright

The unauthorized reproduction or distribution of a copyrighted work is illegal. Criminal copyright infringement, including infringement without monetary gain, is investigated by the FBI and is punishable by fines and federal imprisonment.

Please purchase only authorized editions and do not participate in or encourage, the piracy of copyrighted material. Your support of author's rights is appreciated.

This book is a work of fiction. Names, characters, places and incidents are the products of the author's imagination or used fictitiously. Any resemblance to actual events, locales or persons, living or dead is entirely coincidental.

Copyrighted 2024 by Delta James

❦ Created with Vellum

MERRY CRIS MOOSE
OTTER COVE SHIFTERS

DELTA JAMES

*This book, like all the rest, is dedicated to
My Two Best Friends,
Renee and Chris, without whom none of
what I do would be possible and to the Girls,
who bring joy to my life every single day.*

*And to my readers who love my characters
and stories every bit as much as I do!*

*Acknowledgments As Always to My Team:
Development and Editing: Lori White,
Intuitive Editing and Development Services
Cover Design: Dar Albert, Wicked Smart Designs
Copy Editor/Proofreader: Melinda Kaye Brandt
Beta Readers: Autumn, Kathy, Maggie and Rochelle*

*Leave reality behind and
Welcome to My World!*

KEEP UP WITH DELTA ON SOCIAL MEDIA

Facebook page
Facebook group
Instagram
TikTok
Bookbub
Goodreads
Patreon

Signup for my newsletter and
Get the good stuff...
Each month Delta shares her writing updates, novel releases, exclusive content and some fun personal stories.
Plus - there's often a giveaway!

Thank you!

CHAPTER ONE
KEELY

Otter Cove, Alaska

Keely Blake rushed through the snow-dusted streets of Otter Cove, her boots crunching against the fresh layer of ice beneath her feet. Arms laden with prototype toys, drawings, and schematics, she muttered a string of curses at the biting wind that whipped her auburn hair into a frenzy.

"That's no way for a pretty toy designer to talk," called Zak Grayson as she hurried past him.

"Shut up, Zak," she called good naturedly.

Zak laughed. Zak was the sheriff in Otter Cove and a good friend. He'd recently found his fated mate, Sienna, and the once grumpy sheriff and now seemed to be in a perpetually good mood.

Late again. Why am I always late? Well, this

morning it was because her car had sputtered to a stop two blocks from the office. Her cheeks were flushed both from the cold and her rush to make it to an important meeting on time.

The small town where she had been born and raised was picturesque at any time of year, but during the holiday season the twinkling lights and snow-draped trees made it look like a postcard. Unfortunately, the lovely setting did little to ease the nervous energy knotting in her stomach. Today was important. *'A mysterious new client.'* Her boss' words echoed in her head, and the hint of intrigue only fueled her anxiety. Their clients were usually regional business owners or parents looking for custom toy designs, but if her boss was to be believed, this was big—massive, even.

She knew the company hadn't been doing well, mostly because the current owner, Warren Schultz, was an abysmal businessman. Keely was convinced that the only reason he was the president was because Schultz Toys had been founded by his great, great grandfather and it had always been a privately-owned and run company.

Current rumor had it that Warren was looking to move the company to Seattle or sell it. Either way, Keely felt her days were numbered. At first that had made her angry, but then she'd begun to dream and then to think about going out on her own as a consultant or toy-designer for hire. She didn't know if there was any money to be made, but she loved Otter Cove and couldn't imagine living in the lower forty-eight.

Finally, she reached the small warehouse that served as Schultz Toys' headquarters.

"Morning, Keely," called George, the security man. Security was kind of a misnomer, as she wasn't sure George could keep a kitten out, much less someone intent on physical harm or working to steal company secrets. But still, it was nice to have him around. When she worked late, he often insisted on driving her home.

The warmth of the lobby was a welcome respite from the bitter cold outside. "George, is that CEO guy here?"

"Already in the conference room."

"Shit."

"Not to worry, Keely. You give me your coat and other things. Take a minute to catch your breath and do whatever it is you ladies do in the restroom and then just head in there. I'll make sure the rest of your things get to your office."

He really was a dear man. The fact that he was also a deer-shifter made her smile. "You're the best, George," she said, handing him everything but what she needed for the meeting.

Taking his suggestion, she slipped into the restroom, straightened her clothing, made sure her hair didn't look too much of a mess, pasted on a bright smile, gathered her things and then headed into the conference room. Keely's mind raced as she approached the conference room doors.

She entered through the large glass door and immediately recognized the man with his back turned to her, looking out the large wall of windows onto the harbor. Cris Sutton, CEO of North Star Toys. North Star was a giant in the industry; their toys were unique, well-made, and sold all over the world in the best shops.

Straightening her back, she set her things down on the conference table and then walked around to meet him as he turned to see who'd come through the door.

"Mr. Sutton? I'm Keely Blake. Warren asked me to meet with you. I'm so sorry I'm late."

She was surprised she could get that much out as anything else she might have said was caught in her throat as he extended his hand to her. His pictures did not do the man justice. He was gorgeous—drop dead, jaw dropping, can't speak gorgeous.

Tall and broad-shouldered with dark brown hair, a close-cropped full beard, and intense dark eyes, he exuded a raw, primal energy. His muscular physique, accentuated by his tight-fitting jeans, left little to the imagination, especially when it came to what she was pretty sure was an impressive bulge contained within them. He was the epitome of an alpha male, a role he seemed to embrace with every fiber of his being.

He was mesmerizing, but perhaps it was that he

just seemed to embody every erotic fantasy she'd ever had. His piercing dark eyes locked onto hers, and for a moment, the world seemed to stop spinning. His chiseled features were at odds with the bright, whimsical atmosphere his toy company was known for. No warm smiles or jovial energy here—just raw, dominant, animal magnetism. *Get it together, Keely.*

"Ms. Blake." His voice was low, rough, with a hint of something she couldn't quite place. "I believe you have some designs to show me."

All business. Okay, I can handle that. His gaze flicked briefly to the pile of toys scattered on the table and the drawings laid out haphazardly beside them. Keely suddenly realized how ridiculous she must look—red-faced and snow-dusted with her things scattered across the table. She stifled a nervous laugh.

"Yes, right," she stammered, fumbling to spread out the colorful, handcrafted pieces in a more organized way that would allow him to look at and touch things. Her fingers brushed a small wooden dragon, and she focused on the familiar texture to steady her nerves. "These are my latest prototypes—interactive toys for kids. I designed them to inspire creativity and adventure." She lifted her eyes to meet his, but Cris's expression remained unreadable. "Our IT department is working on a program where kids can scan their toys into an interactive game."

Keely's heart thudded in her chest as she continued, describing the intricate details of each toy. But Cris wasn't looking at the toys. No, his gaze kept returning to her—intense and unwavering, as if he were studying her every move, every breath. It was as if she could feel the weight of that gaze, her pulse quickening under his scrutiny. There was something about him that pulled her in despite the gruff demeanor he projected.

"Interesting," Cris said after a long moment, his voice sending a shiver down her spine. "Your designs are... imaginative."

He was known as a man of few words who played his cards close to his vest. North Star Toys was located in a remote area to the north. Very few details were known about the company, other than it was a leader in the toy industry and that those who worked for them rarely, if ever, left. A compliment coming from him meant something to Keely. But it wasn't just the words, it was the heat in his gaze that sent another, entirely different surge of energy coursing through her system.

"Thank you," she said, her voice soft, betraying the tension that was building between them. She hadn't expected this. Hadn't expected him.

He stepped closer, his imposing frame seeming to fill the space, and the air between them felt charged, crackling with an unspoken attraction neither could deny. Cris's eyes softened ever so slightly, but his voice remained steady. "I like what I see. You've put a lot of thought into these designs. I can see your passion for what you do. Too bad Warren Schultz is a fool. I came to see your designs, but my ulterior motive was to meet you."

"Me?"

He nodded. "You."

Keely's breath caught. There was something in the way he said it that made her think he wasn't just talking about her work. Her mind raced, torn between professionalism and the growing tension in the room. She couldn't ignore it—the way he was looking at her, the subtle electricity that hummed between them like an undercurrent of desire.

Their eyes met, and for a moment, everything else disappeared. The room, the toys, the snow falling gently outside. It was just her and Cris, standing far too close for this to be a normal business meeting.

"Your company's reputation for cheerful design and quality workmanship..." she began, trying to keep the conversation on track, but her voice wavered as he stepped even closer. "You're not exactly what I was expecting, if I'd been expecting you at all."

"Oh?" he asked, arching a dark eyebrow at her.

"Warren didn't give me specifics. He just told me I would be meeting with a new prospective client."

"Knowing Schultz, he told you I could be a 'big' client."

She grinned. She didn't know what else to say. She was too aware of how close he had come, how his scent—a mix of cedar and something darker—filled the air between them. Her skin prickled with awareness, and she wondered if he felt it too, this undeniable pull between them. It was probably all in her mind. He was most likely happily married. She snuck a glance at his ring finger—nothing there, not even a tan line. The tension was almost unbearable now, the room feeling too small, too intimate.

"Would it surprise you to know North Star tried to buy Schultz toys?"

"Yes. Yes, it would," she stammered.

"Schultz wouldn't sell. Well, that's not true, but he wanted to sell at more than twice what the company is worth. My people tried to tell me if you were part of the deal, it would be worth it. My current head designer, Tinker, said if I saw your toys in person, I'd be hooked. He was right. So instead of buying the company, I guess I'll have to settle for buying its toys and perhaps getting to know its head designer better."

Keely's breath caught in her throat, her heart thudding against her ribcage as she met his gaze, her pulse racing with a mix of excitement and anticipation. She knew she should step back, put some space between them, but she couldn't. She didn't want to. The intensity in his eyes, the raw magnetism of his presence—it was intoxicating.

If Warren really was trying to sell the company or move it south, Cris Sutton and North Star Toys might just be her first client. The weight of Cris's words seemed to be heavy with unspoken promises. Promises she was sure she was imagining. His dark eyes remained locked on hers, and for a moment, she couldn't move—could barely breathe under the intensity of his gaze. Her mind spun, searching for something to break the tension, but nothing came. Every thought, every professional boundary, evaporated in the heat of the moment.

"Dinner," Cris said abruptly, his deep voice slicing through the thick air. It wasn't a question, but the command wasn't harsh, either. "Tonight." He shook his head, grinning. "That came out rather harsh. Let me try again. I'd like to take you to dinner."

Keely blinked, her pulse spiking in disbelief. This wasn't happening, was it? The CEO of North Star Toys was asking her out? Her heart raced, and her common sense struggled to catch up with her desire.

She swallowed hard, trying to find her footing. "Dinner?" she repeated, as if she hadn't heard him right the first time. It felt like such a normal word in the middle of all the electricity swirling between them.

Cris's lips quirked into the faintest hint of a smile, his gaze never leaving hers. "Yes, Keely. Dinner. You know, that meal in the evening where you eat? Dinner. Tonight. Are you interested?"

There was a certainty in his tone, an assurance that made her heart flutter. But the way he said her name sent shivers down her spine. Every part of her wanted to say yes, even though she knew it was a bad idea, even though she could already feel herself stepping past the line of professionalism. She should decline, she really should—but that magnetic pull was too strong.

"I'd like that," she said softly, her words hanging in the charged air between them.

His smile deepened, satisfaction glinting in his eyes as if he had known what her answer would be all along. "Good. I'll pick you up at seven."

Keely's head was spinning long after Cris left the conference room. Her body still hummed with the tension that had built between them, and as the day passed in a haze of nervous anticipation, she couldn't focus on anything but what awaited her tonight.

She went back to her office in something of a haze and then left early. She hadn't been on a date in months, maybe longer. She needed to go for a run, get cleaned up, wash her hair, shave all the necessary parts, and figure out what the hell she was going to wear to dinner with the sexiest man she'd ever met.

CHAPTER TWO

KEELY

The mid-afternoon sun hung low in the Alaskan sky, casting a golden light over the snow-covered landscape. It was the time of day Keely loved most—when the world seemed to glow with an ethereal warmth, despite the biting cold that always lingered in the air. Her sleek, white fox form moved effortlessly through the snow, her paws light, barely disturbing the surface as she ran. This was her sanctuary, where she could think, where she could let go.

But today, her thoughts weren't as free as they usually were. Her mind kept wandering back to the man she'd met earlier that day—Cris Sutton. There was something about him—something beyond how gorgeous, dominant, and sexy he was. Something about the way he seemed so comfortable in the conference room while at the same time giving the air of someone who would be comfortable in any environment. Something that felt... familiar.

She continued to run and then slid to a stop. Could Cris be like her? Like everyone in Otter Cove? A shifter? Was everyone at North Star a shifter, too?

She tried to shake the idea from her mind, knowing that she was just projecting her own desires onto the man. But as she thought back to their meeting, she realized there had been subtle clues—his keen sense of awareness, the way he had seemed to anticipate her movements when they'd spoken. And then there was the moment when their hands brushed, and she'd felt the faintest hint of energy pass between them, something only another shifter could sense.

Keely picked up her pace and headed back to her cabin, her fox form dissolving in a swirling mist as she entered and shifted back into her human body. Her dark hair cascaded down her back, and she stood barefoot in her kitchen, lost in thought. She shivered slightly as the chilled air kissed her skin.

Cris Sutton. The more she thought about it, the surer she became he was a shifter. Could he be like her? Maybe not a fox, but something else. A wolf? A bear? Or perhaps something else altogether. If Cris was a shifter, it would explain the connection she'd felt. And yet, she wasn't sure if she was ready to confront him, to ask. Revealing her own nature was risky, even to someone who might share it.

The warmth of the indoors began to seep into her body, chasing away the chill, but her thoughts of Cris —of what he might be—lingered, unresolved. Before heading into the shower, she grabbed her robe and checked her computer. An email from Warren. Taking a deep breath and exhaling it slowly, she opened it.

Subject: Important Company Update
Keely,
I wanted to inform you ahead of the official announcement that Schultz's Toys has been sold to Vanguard Holdings. We will be undergoing significant changes in the coming months, including restructuring of our design team. I know this may come as a shock, but we'll provide more details soon.
Best regards,
Warren Schultz

Vanguard? That soulless shell of a company? Keely guessed she didn't need to worry about whether or not she would try and show Cris Sutton some of her own designs. Most of the things she'd shown him today were part of her work at

Schultz Toys, but Warren had hated the dragon and had refused to put money into her idea about an interactive program. The IT guys, however, had loved the idea and had been working on it on their own time. Her plan had been, once it was ready, to show it to Warren again and hope he would get behind it. If Cris liked it, maybe she could sell it to North Star instead.

Later, as she stood in front of the antique floor mirror, Keely couldn't remember the last time she had felt this jittery, smoothing the wrinkles from her little black dress. It had been a splurge the last time she'd been in Seattle. It had called her name from a Nordstrom's window display, and she had heeded its siren's call. Her reflection stared back at her, wide-eyed, a mix of nerves and excitement bubbling inside her chest.

She told herself she was a vision of feminine allure. Her dark auburn hair framed her face, highlighting her sparkling eyes and full, pink lips. Her curves were accentuated by the figure-hugging dress that showcased her hourglass shape, with ample cleavage on display. She had a playful, adventurous spirit that seemed to have taken over from the moment she laid eyes on Cris.

Her nerves were brushed away when she answered the door. His eyes lit up, and he said, "Wow. Just wow."

The evening started innocently enough, and dinner

was delicious and tantalizing, filled with a subtle undercurrent of heat that left her mind in a fog. Otter Cove might be a small town, but the Otter Cove Inn had an excellent restaurant. As they ate, she couldn't help occasionally glancing at Cris's lap and had to stop herself from licking her lips. She wondered if he had any idea that she relished the thought of submitting to a man like him as the women did in the romance novels she loved, especially the ones with dominant men.

As he walked her to the door, Keely decided to do something out of character for her, hoping that if she made the first move, he would pick up the ball and run with it.

"Would you like to come in for a glass of wine?" she asked as she unlocked the door.

"I'm not much of a wine drinker," Cris said, his deep voice filling the space around them. "I prefer something with a bit more kick."

Keely's eyes lit up with mischief. "Oh, I think I might have just the thing. I've got some local microbrews in the fridge. They're quite strong, but they go down smoothly."

Cris raised an eyebrow, intrigued. "Sounds perfect. Lead the way, beautiful."

She led him inside. The cozy atmosphere of Keely's cabin was the perfect setting for a drink and maybe more. The cabin, with its charm and warm wooden tones, seemed to envelop them in a sensual embrace as soon as they stepped inside.

Feeling a surge of arousal, she led Cris into the kitchen. The cabin's open floor plan meant the kitchen was just a few steps away, and the rustic, wooden countertops and shelves added to the intimate ambiance. She reached into the fridge and pulled out two bottles, their labels promising a potent brew.

It started with a kiss—she'd stood up from grabbing the microbrews to find him standing right behind her. His lips had brushed hers, soft at first, testing, then firmer as he deepened it, pulling her close with a possessiveness that left her weak at the knees. Keely's heart raced as his hands slid down her sides, his touch setting her skin on fire through her thin, black dress.

Somewhere in the back of her mind, she knew this was moving fast, too fast, but her overwhelming arousal and need to be with him drowned out her logic. Cris's mouth on her neck, his fingers tangling in her hair, his breath warm against her ear—it was all too much. She had wanted him from the moment she'd laid eyes on him, and now, here they were, the desire between them tangible and undeniable.

When he lifted his head, she handed him a bottle, their fingers touched, and a spark of electricity shot through them both. Cris's eyes narrowed, and a sultry grin lifted the corners of his mouth as he took it, his fingers brushing against hers deliberately. He twisted off the cap and took a long swallow.

"Mmm, that hits the spot," he murmured, his voice low and husky. "Careful, it's strong."

Keely took a tentative sip, her eyes widening at the powerful flavor. "I know. I'm the one who gave it to you. Kind of hits you like a freight train, doesn't it?"

Cris stepped closer, his body invading her personal space. "Hard, fast, and leaves you a little breathless," he whispered, his breath hot against her ear.

Keely shivered, her nipples hardening against the fabric of her dress. She turned to face him, her eyes locking with his. "Hard, fast, and breathless. I think I'd like that," she said, her voice steady despite the desire coursing through her veins. Keely's heart raced as she imagined Cris taking her from behind, his powerful body driving into her.

Cris's grin grew wider, and he placed his bottle on the counter with deliberate slowness. "Would you now? I think I can accommodate that."

He didn't wait for her to answer but took her microbrew, set it on the counter, then tossed her over his shoulder and carried her into the bedroom. It helped that the bedroom was right off the kitchen through a large, open archway. Her antique brass bed, with its colorful quilt, beckoned to them.

Cris laid Keely down on the bed, his eyes never leaving hers. Standing over her, the chandelier that hung over her bed cast a shadow of his muscular frame across her body. He slowly began to undress. Keely's breath caught in her throat as she watched him reveal his broad shoulders, chiseled torso, muscular arms, and rippling abs. His hands went to his belt, and with a swift motion, he unbuckled it, letting his jeans slide down his thighs, revealing black boxer briefs that strained to contain his impressive erection.

"Oh my god, you're gorgeous," Keely breathed, her eyes fixed on the bulge in his underwear.

Cris chuckled, a deep, rumbling sound. "No, baby, you're the one who's beautiful, all wrapped up in that dress like a pretty present I've been wanting to open all night."

He stepped out of his jeans and kicked them aside, then hooked his thumbs under the waistband of his briefs, slowly lowering them, revealing his thick, veined cock. It stood proudly, already glistening with pre-cum at the tip. Keely's mouth watered at the sight, and she licked her lips in anticipation.

"You're huge," she whispered, her eyes wide.

Cris crawled onto the bed, his eyes never leaving hers as he loomed over her. "No, baby, I'm just the right size to fill you up."

Keely's heart was pounding in her chest, her body trembling with desire. She wanted to feel every inch of him inside her, to be claimed by this powerful man.

She spread her legs invitingly, her dress riding up her thighs, revealing her lace panties.

Cris leaned down, his lips capturing hers in a passionate kiss. His tongue invaded her mouth, demanding and possessive, mirroring the way she was sure he intended to take her body. Keely moaned into his mouth, her hands threading through his hair, pulling him closer. She could taste the beer on his tongue, mixed with the wild, primal essence of the man himself.

Cris broke the kiss, trailing hot, open-mouthed kisses down her neck, leaving a trail of wetness and desire. His hands roamed over her body, cupping her breasts, squeezing and kneading them through the fabric of her dress. Keely arched her back, pushing her chest into his hands, craving more.

With a swift motion, Cris removed the dress from her body, leaving her in just her lace panties and bra. He unhooked her bra with nimble fingers, freeing her full, heavy breasts. Keely's nipples were already hard and aching, the peaks dark and swollen. Cris bent down and took one nipple into his mouth, sucking and teasing it with his tongue, while his fingers pinched and rolled the other.

Keely moaned in absolute ecstasy—this was the kind of thing she'd always dreamed about.

Cris lavished attention on her sensitive buds, his mouth and fingers working in tandem to drive her wild. Keely's hands gripped the sheets, her hips undulating as waves of pleasure coursed through her.

"Fuck, your nipples are sweet," Cris murmured against her skin. "Let's see how the rest of you tastes."

Cris hooked his fingers under the waistband of her panties and slowly slid them down her legs, his eyes feasting on her naked form. He made a place for himself between her legs, burying his face between her thighs, his tongue finding her clit, swirling and flicking it with expert precision. Keely's hips bucked wildly as she cried out, her juices flowing freely, coating Cris's tongue and beard.

"That's it, baby, come for me," he growled, his voice muffled against her pussy.

Keely's orgasm hit her like an avalanche, her body shaking uncontrollably as she called his name, tangling her fingers in his hair. He lapped at her eagerly, drinking in her essence, his tongue never slowing until she was writhing and spent.

"That was incredible," she panted, her eyes glazed with pleasure.

Cris smiled, his face glistening with her juices. "We're just getting started, sweetheart. Now, it's my turn."

He moved back up her body—kissing, licking, and nipping as he went until he positioned himself between her legs, his thick shaft pressing against her wet slit. Keely spread herself wide, eager for him to fill her. With one powerful thrust, Cris buried himself deep inside her, possessing her completely.

Giving her a moment to adjust to his size, Cris then began to move, his hips pumping in a steady rhythm, his cock sliding in and out of her slick heat. He gripped her thighs, spreading her wide, giving him even deeper access. Keely's eyes rolled back in her head as pleasure overwhelmed her, her nails digging into his back as she clung to him.

"You like that, don't you, baby?" Cris growled, his voice rough with desire.

Keely was too far gone to manage words, so she moaned.

Taking that for a yes, Cris obliged, picking up the pace, his hips slamming into hers with abandon. The bed creaked and groaned with each powerful thrust, the headboard banging against the wall, adding to the erotic symphony. Keely's body trembled, her orgasm building again, fueled by the intensity of their coupling.

"Come with me, Keely," Cris grunted, his breath coming in short, sharp gasps. "I want to feel your pussy milk my cock."

Keely's body tightened around him, her inner walls pulsing and clenching as another orgasm ripped through her. Cris roared as he felt her climax, his own release building to an explosive peak. With one final, powerful thrust, he emptied himself into her, his hot cum filling her up, their bodies moving as one in a symphony of ecstasy.

They lay entangled in each other's arms, their hearts racing and their bodies slick with sweat and cum. The evening's passion had been more intense than either of them had anticipated, but it was exactly what they both needed.

As they caught their breath, Keely smiled up at Cris, her eyes sparkling with contentment. "That was... incredible. I've never been fucked like that before."

Cris grinned, his dark eyes gleaming with satisfaction. "Glad to be of service, beautiful. And I'm not done with you yet. I plan on making you come a few more times before the night is through."

Keely's eyes widened, a mixture of excitement and anticipation. "Oh, I can't wait. But first, I think we should finish those beers. I have a feeling we're both going to need them."

They laughed. It was clear that this night was just the beginning of something fiery and wild. It was like nothing she'd ever experienced—intense, primal, and overwhelming. Cris was dominant, commanding, his movements confident, and every moment left her gasping for more. The cabin was filled with the sounds of their passion, the world outside forgotten.

K eely awoke slowly the next morning, the warmth of the soft sheets surrounding her as the early morning light filtered through her curtains. For a moment, she lay still, her body still humming from the night before, a languid satisfaction settling in her bones.

But when she reached out beside her, the space next to her was empty. The sheets were cold, the imprint of his body already fading.

Her heart sank, an uneasy feeling creeping up her chest. She sat up, pulling the sheet around her as she looked around the room. The clothes that had been strewn across the floor were gone, and there, on the nightstand, a small note sat folded neatly.

Keely's stomach twisted as she reached for it, her fingers trembling slightly as she unfolded the paper.

Keely, something urgent came up. I had to leave early. Last night was... unexpected, but I don't regret it. I'll be in touch. - Cris.

She stared at the words, her mind trying to process the mixed emotions swirling inside her. *I'll be in touch?* The casual tone of it stung more than she expected. Was this just a fling to him? A one-night indulgence in the middle of his business trip? Well, what had she expected? It wasn't like she'd made it difficult for him.

Aggravated, she tossed the note back on the nightstand, pulling the sheet tighter around her as she stared at the empty bed. What had she been thinking? Letting herself get swept away like that, caught up in the intensity of it all. Now, in the quiet light of morning, the high from their encounter had faded, leaving only questions—and an ache she hadn't anticipated. She had no idea where things stood between them now, but one thing was certain: Cris Sutton had walked out of her life as quickly as he had entered it, leaving her with nothing but confusion and the lingering warmth of his touch.

CHAPTER
THREE
CRIS

Cris strode through the thick snow, his breath coming out in quick clouds as he crossed the icy courtyard of North Star's Headquarters. His coat was pulled tight around him, but the cold did little to numb the heat still coursing through his veins—the lingering fire left behind from his night with Keely. He couldn't stop thinking about her. The reality of his world and all it entailed had yanked him away far too soon.

He clenched his fists as he neared the towering doors of the North Star Toy factory, frustration gnawing at him. He hadn't wanted to leave like that, slipping out before dawn with only a note to explain. If it hadn't been for that urgent message from Holly, his chief toymaker, he might still be there with Keely, tangled in her sheets, exploring every inch of her until they both forgot about the outside world.

But Holly's message had been clear: something was wrong. Something was very wrong.

The heavy wooden doors swung open, the warm glow from inside spilling into the snow-covered courtyard. The scent of gingerbread and peppermint always lingered in the air here, but today, there seemed to be a subtle change in the magic that pulsed through the place.

Holly was waiting for him just inside the entrance, her petite figure tense, a frown creasing her usually cheerful face. Being an elf, Holly's pointed ears twitched slightly when something had her rattled.

"Holly," Cris said as he approached, his voice rougher than usual. His thoughts were still half-occupied with Keely, but the seriousness in Holly's eyes snapped his focus back to the present. "What's going on?"

"It's bad, Cris," Holly said, her green eyes wide with concern. She shifted nervously, her small hands clasped together. "We've been keeping a close eye on the belief levels around the world. They're dropping... fast."

A cold dread slid through him. "How fast?" he asked, his jaw tightening. She was right; they had been watching them, but he hadn't anticipated this, not so soon before Christmas.

"Way too fast." Holly shook her head, her voice dropping to a whisper. "If they keep dropping, we might not have enough to keep up with production, much less to power the sleigh. We've tried recalibrating the distribution systems, but it isn't doing any good. It's like with fewer and fewer people believing, the magic is... fading."

Cris cursed under his breath, running a hand through his hair. "This can't be happening," he muttered. "Not now."

"We have to figure this out. If we don't, we'll be lucky to get through the season. I can't imagine a world without Christmas and all the magic that comes with it."

Cris nodded and gestured for her to follow as they made their way through the open workshop and into the main meeting hall. The place was usually bustling with activity—elves working on the latest toys, the hum of the season filling the air—but today, the energy felt subdued. Even the overhead lights seemed dimmer, flickering slightly as if struggling to stay lit.

Damn it.

His thoughts raced as he walked, feeling the weight of his responsibilities. This was more than just a job. For him and everyone else here, Christmas had become something of a calling. It had been ever since Santa entrusted him with overseeing the operations at

North Star Toys. He needed to get this fixed, and fast, before it reached Santa's ears.

Pushing the door to the conference room open, Cris found Jack and Tinker already waiting for him. Jack leaned casually against the wall, his pale skin and silver hair making him look as frosty as the winter air outside, but there was a sharpness in his gaze, an awareness of the gravity of the situation. Tinker, the head of the toy division, sat at the table, his brow furrowed as he toyed with a small mechanical gadget in his hands.

"This had better be good, Cris," Jack drawled, his eyes narrowing. "I was in the middle of a rather important ice storm."

"I'm not in the mood, Jack," Cris snapped as he took his place at the head of the table. "We have a serious problem. Holly says the belief levels are dropping all over the world. If we don't get it fixed, Christmas could be in jeopardy."

Tinker frowned, setting down the gadget. "The belief levels? That hasn't happened in—well, in at least the last couple of centuries." He turned to Holly. "Any idea what's causing it?"

"None. I've been over all the data and it makes no sense."

"I had to go south to meet with the head toy designer of Schultz Toys..."

"Keely Blake?" asked Tinker, his head coming up.

"Oh, she's good. Very good. Her toys might have just that spark needed to make the kids' belief systems go into overdrive."

"That was my thought, as well," said Cris, nodding. "Holly and her people have done everything they could," he said drumming his fingers on the table.

"Nothing is working," Holly admitted. "I'm really afraid we're running out of time."

"Not to worry," said Jack. "The head honcho is back; I'm sure he'll figure it out."

Tinker shifted in his seat. "But belief doesn't just vanish like that. Something—or *someone*—has to be draining it."

"Agreed," said Cris, frustration gnawing at him. "We need to figure out what's happening and get it stopped before it's too late."

Holly stepped forward, her voice quiet but firm. "If the world is losing its belief in Christmas and everything it stands for, we might not have enough magic to finish making the toys or to power Santa's sleigh. The reindeer can help with Christmas Eve and the way they manipulate time, but there's nothing else they can do."

The room went silent, the air heavy and thick with tension as everyone exchanged uneasy glances. Cris could feel the weight of their gazes on him, waiting for direction, for answers. But he didn't have any. It didn't help that his mind kept drifting back to

Keely. Something about her still lingered in his thoughts.

"Cris?" Tinker's voice broke through his thoughts. "We need a plan."

Feeling the weight of responsibility on his shoulders, Cris straightened his back. "First things first," he said, his voice steady. "We need to isolate the problem. Holly, you and Tinker focus on the factory's reserves. Look for any anomalies in the system, anything that could point to why the power levels are dropping so rapidly. Jack..."

"I'll handle the external factors," Jack interrupted, his eyes locked on Cris. "I'll check the weather patterns to see if there's any unusual activity in the northern realms. If someone's tampering with something, it won't go unnoticed."

Cris nodded, grateful for Jack's willingness to take this seriously. With Jack that wasn't always a given. "Good. I'll keep an eye on production levels and the sleigh. If things don't get better fast, we might need to prepare for the worst."

"And what about Santa?" Holly asked, her voice hesitant. "He's going to find out sooner or later."

"Not if we can help it," Cris said firmly. "The big guy's got enough on his plate. This is our problem to solve."

The room fell silent; the enormity of the situation sinking in. Cris's mind churned with possibilities, strategies, and the growing fear of what might happen if they didn't figure out what was happening in time.

As the meeting broke up and he headed for his cabin, his mind drifted back to Keely. He needed to see her again. Maybe Tinker was right. Maybe she could help. Or maybe he was just trying to justify reaching out to her.

He let out a breath, trying to steady himself, but a chill of realization crawled down his spine. Keely wasn't just some woman. She was *his* woman. The thought hit him with the force of a sledgehammer, making his heart pounded in his chest. *Fated mate.* He hadn't believed it could happen—not to him. Fated mates happened to predators—lions, tigers, wolves and the like, but not to non-predatory species like him. While moose could be lethal, they were not in the same class as the more overtly violent species. They were, however, incredibly pragmatic, and Cris took great pride in that. He had accepted that his role as Santa's right-hand man would mean sacrifices. Family, love—those things had never been part of his plan.

Until now.

As he poured himself a cup of coffee, his mind was spinning, piecing together the sudden connection that was forming in his head. *Keely's toy designs.* They had been brilliant, filled with whimsy and imagination—exactly the kind of thing that could spark belief in children. And belief, more than anything, was the lifeblood of Christmas magic.

It was a long shot, but what if Keely's innovative creations were the key to reigniting belief? What if *she* was the answer to the crisis they were facing?

He picked up his phone and dialed Tinker. "Tinker, what if we brought on a whole new line of toys?"

"That's not so easily done, especially this time of year. Most designers are finishing up their work."

"What about Keely Blake?"

"She works for Schultz..."

"But what if she didn't? I got the feeling she was holding something back. What if she's been developing her own line of toys?"

There was silence on the other end. "Maybe. Her designs are different. They're... innovative, filled with something that's missing in other toys—even ours. The kind of things that could remind children of the magic and wonder they've been losing touch with. If we can introduce her ideas into production, it might be enough to reverse the decline."

"It's a risk," Cris said, his voice cautious. "Bringing someone here—letting them in on what's really going on... it's dangerous. What if she can't handle it?"

"She can. She lives in Otter Cove. Either she's a shifter, or she at least understands the need for secrecy," Tinker said firmly. "It's a small step from that to believing in magic... just ask Dash."

What Tinker didn't know, but Cris did, was that she was his fated mate. None of them needed to know that—not even Keely. She might not be aware, but she had to have felt the connection even if she didn't completely understand it. He wasn't about to let her slip through his fingers—especially not when she could be the key to saving everything.

"Then it's settled. I'm bringing her here," Cris said, his tone brooking no argument. "I think she's our best bet."

"Agreed," said Tinker. "If we don't find a way to stabilize things soon, we won't have a Christmas to save."

He would go to Keely. He would bring her here. And he would face whatever consequences came with it. Because something deep inside him told him that she was more than just a brilliant designer. She was the answer to everything.

CHAPTER
FOUR
KEELY

Keely sat in the center of her workroom, the soft glow of Christmas lights twinkling in the windows as the cold wind howled outside her cabin. The familiar tools of her trade surrounded her: bits of wood, screws, metal scraps, soldering irons and tiny gears strewn across the workbench. She should have been focusing on the final touches of her latest prototype—a mechanical elf that waved and played holiday songs—but her mind was far from the toy in front of her.

Instead, it kept wandering back to Cris Sutton.

With a frustrated sigh, she set her carving tool down and rubbed her temples. The design had been due days ago, but every time she tried to concentrate, thoughts of Cris clouded her mind, sending a wave of heat through her body that left her restless and unfocused. She hadn't been able to shake the memory of their night together—his touch, his scent, the way he had made her feel as though she were the only thing that mattered in the world.

But then he had left. Without a word, slipping out of her bed before dawn with nothing but a hastily written note as an apology.

Keely exhaled sharply, trying to push the memory aside. She couldn't afford to get distracted by Cris Sutton. Not now, with her career on the line. She wasn't going to work for Vanguard. She'd given her notice, and this last prototype was the last thing she owed them. Warren had whined and said Vanguard wanted to keep her on, but Keely was ready to forge her own path, and she wasn't about to let some enigmatic CEO derail her focus.

Just as she was about to force herself back to work, the sound of her phone buzzing on the workbench broke the silence. Keely glanced over at the screen, her breath catching when she saw his name flash across it.

Cris Sutton.

A video call.

Her heart skipped a beat, and her fingers hovered over the phone, hesitation gripping her. Part of her wanted to ignore it—to let him wait, just like he had left her waiting after their night together. But the more professional part of her whispered that this was business. She couldn't just ignore a potential client, even if he had left her feeling confused and a little hurt.

She sighed and tapped the screen, accepting the call.

"Keely," Cris's deep voice resonated through the speaker before his face appeared on the screen. His dark eyes locked onto hers through the phone, and for a moment, she forgot how to breathe. Even over video, his presence was undeniable. His dark hair was slightly mussed, as though he had been running his hands through it, and the sharp line of his jaw was clenched in a way that made her heart stutter.

She quickly composed herself, lifting her chin. "Mr. Sutton. What can I do for you?" Her tone was cool, professional, despite the rush of emotions swirling inside her.

He exhaled, his expression softening just slightly. "'Mr. Sutton?' I suppose I deserve that, at least from your point of view. I know you probably don't want to hear from me right now, but I need to explain. I didn't mean to leave like that."

Keely narrowed her eyes, crossing her arms in front of her. "You didn't *mean* to? What exactly did you mean? What, Cris? You just happened to disappear without a word?"

He ran a hand through his hair, his frustration evident. "I didn't want to leave. Trust me, I would have stayed if I could, but something urgent came up—

something I couldn't ignore. It wasn't personal, Keely. I didn't want you to think... I left you a note," he finished lamely.

He trailed off, the weight of his words hanging in the air between them. Keely's chest tightened as she watched him struggle for an explanation. Part of her wanted to believe him, but another part of her was still reeling from how abruptly he had left.

"And I'm just supposed to believe that?" she said, her voice quieter now, less certain. "You vanish with nothing more than a note, then not a word, and now... what? You're suddenly back in my life like that night never happened?"

Cris's gaze softened, and his voice dropped, as if the distance between them mattered less than what he had to say. "Keely, I'm sorry. That's all I can say. I read this morning that Schultz sold out to Vanguard Holdings. Are you going to stay?"

"I don't know that that's any of your business."

"It might not be if I wasn't calling you to offer you a job."

A job? Did I hear him right? Keely's resolve wavered as she looked at him, feeling the pull of his sincerity, the apology in his dark eyes. She knew she should stay firm, that she couldn't let him off the hook so easily—but damn it, he made it so hard to think clearly. Her fingers flexed against the workbench, trying to grasp at some semblance of control.

"A job?" she asked finally, her voice steadying as she forced herself to meet his gaze. "I'm listening."

Cris's expression shifted slightly, a flicker of relief passing through his features. "I need your help. Your designs—they're incredible, Keely. They have a kind of magic to them that's more than just craftsmanship. And right now, I'm facing a situation that I believe your ideas could solve. I want to offer you a consulting contract. I'd offer just to hire you, but I'm worried you'd turn me down."

"What makes you think I won't?"

"Because I'll make it worth your while. And if you're going to go out on your own, having a client like North Star Toys would help. And if you decide you like it, you could pretty much dictate your terms."

Keely frowned, skepticism rising in her. "I thought you already had a team of designers. I don't want to get anyone fired or demoted."

"That's the furthest thing from my mind," Cris said, his voice growing more urgent, "This is bigger than just toys. I need someone with your unique perspective—someone who can think outside the box. You've got an eye for innovation that we don't see every day, and I believe you could make a real difference."

She blinked, her heart pounding as she tried to process what he was saying. This was unexpected—more than just a simple apology or an attempt to explain away their night together. This was business. Real business.

But something about the way he said it, the intensity in his voice, made her feel like there was more to it than just work.

"And what exactly are you asking me to do?" she asked, narrowing her gaze slightly. "Because I'm not interested in being strung along, Cris—personally or professionally. If this is just some way to—"

"It's not," he interrupted quickly. "This is serious. And it's not just some remote job. I want to bring you to the North Pole."

Keely blinked in surprise, her mouth opening but no words coming out. *The North Pole?* He couldn't be serious.

Cris continued, sensing her shock. "I know how it sounds, but I'm not joking. This isn't a game, Keely. I'm not going to lie to you. We're facing a crisis—a real one—and your designs, your ideas, might be the key to fixing it. I don't want to sound too dramatic, but I think we need you to save Christmas."

Keely felt her heart skip a beat at the absurdity of it. Christmas? *Saving Christmas?* It sounded like something straight out of a children's book, but the gravity in his voice told her he wasn't playing around. He believed what he was saying.

"And you think my toy designs are going to fix this

crisis?" she asked, her voice laced with disbelief, but curiosity tugged at her.

"I do. And so does Tinker." Tinker was a legend in the toy design business. "We can discuss the specifics once you get here," Cris said, leaning closer to the screen, his dark eyes as intense ever. "All I'm asking is that you give me a few days and trust me. I can explain everything once you're here, and I promise—it'll be worth it. I'll pay you upfront for thirty days, and you only have to agree to come. Once you step off the plane, you can leave any time you like."

She stared at him, torn between disbelief and the strange pull he had over her. Going to the North Pole? Consulting on some mysterious project that involved saving Christmas? It was ludicrous—and yet, the way he was looking at her, the urgency in his voice... something said this was more than just a job offer.

Before she knew what she was doing, the words slipped out. "When do I leave?"

Cris's eyes softened, and a small smile tugged at the corner of his mouth. "Tomorrow. Pack warm."

Keely hung up the call, staring at her phone in stunned silence. What had she just agreed to? Going to the North Pole, to work with Cris on some secret project? The rational part of her screamed that this was a terrible idea, but deep down, something else simmered. Something that had been building ever since their night together.

Whatever was happening, it felt bigger than her—and she wasn't about to back down from it.

∽

Later, Keely sat cross-legged on her couch, twirling the edge of her blanket in her fingers as she stared at her phone. The video call with Cris earlier in the day had left her buzzing with so many conflicting emotions. The idea of going to the North Pole? It was absurd. Ridiculous, even. And yet... she couldn't stop the thrill that coursed through her at the thought of being near him again. His dark eyes had drawn her in even through the screen, full of intensity and something more—something she couldn't quite put her finger on.

She groaned and buried her face in her hands. Slowly she picked up the phone and called Sienna Grayson, the sheriff's mate. She briefly explained everything that had happened, finishing with, "What am I even thinking?"

"It sounds to me like you're thinking about a hunky CEO and forging a new path for yourself."

"But that's crazy, isn't it?"

"Well, there's crazy, and then there's crazy. This sounds like the good kind of crazy."

Keely felt her cheeks flush as she remembered the heat of their night together. The way his touch had set her skin on fire, the way his lips had moved against hers with a raw hunger that still left her breathless. "It was just... one night."

"One *very* passionate night, and sometimes all it takes is one night. Don't even try to tell me you don't want more of Mr. Cris Sutton. Push comes to shove, you go up there, fuck his brains out, take his money, and leave *him* a note."

Keely sighed, burying her face in the blanket again. "There's something about him... something that pulls me in, and I can't explain it. It's like I'm being drawn to him, even though I know I should be more cautious. It almost makes me nauseous to think about it... him."

"Nauseous? Dizzy? Disoriented?"

"Yeah. That's not good, right?"

"Depends on how you feel about finding your fated mate."

"No."

"Yes," said Sienna, laughing.

"Oh lord," said Keely as Sienna continued to laugh. "I guess I'm going to the North Pole. I don't know what's waiting for me there, but I'm done playing it safe. I need to take a chance."

"That's my girl! And who knows? Maybe you'll come back with more than just a new job. I'm sensing some serious 'romance of the century' vibes here."

Keely laughed despite herself. There was something bigger at play here, and she couldn't shake the feeling that stepping into Cris's world was about to change everything.

~

T he next day, Keely found herself standing at the small private airport just outside of town, her suitcase in hand, staring at a sleek private jet with the North Star Toys logo emblazoned on the side. The chill in the air was sharp, biting at her skin, but it was nothing compared to the nervous energy buzzing inside her.

What was she even doing? This was madness. She was about to board a jet to the North Pole, to work on a mysterious project with a man who made her heart race in ways she hadn't thought possible. A man, she reminded herself, who had left her bed without a word but had somehow pulled her into his orbit with such force that she couldn't seem to break free.

The jet door opened, and a flight attendant smiled warmly at her. "Ms. Blake, we're ready for you."

Keely nodded, her heart pounding in her chest. She took a deep breath and stepped onto the jet, her mind swirling with uncertainty and anticipation. This was it. She was leaving everything behind—her job, her life, her comfort zone—and stepping into a world she knew very little about.

As the jet's engines roared to life and the plane

began to roll down the runway and lift off, Keely gazed out the window, watching the ground fall away beneath her. Her breath caught in her throat, a mixture of excitement and fear rushing through her.

Whatever awaited her at the North Pole, she knew one thing for sure—there was no turning back now.

CHAPTER
FIVE
CRIS

Cris paced along the edge of the North Pole's airstrip, his breath forming soft puffs of fog in the crisp, frigid air as snowflakes drifted down lazily from the sky. His boots crunched against the frozen ground, his body humming with a nervous energy he hadn't felt in what seemed like forever. He'd faced countless crises, managed the magic of Christmas through storm and strife, yet the idea of bringing her here, to this sacred, hidden world, set him on edge in ways he wasn't prepared for.

The swirling storm of thoughts in his mind made him doubt his decision. What was he thinking? Bringing someone he barely knew—but was that really true? Didn't it feel like he'd known her all his life and had just been waiting for her to arrive?—to the North Pole, the very heart of what most people thought of as Christmas? Bringing in outsiders was rare. There were strict rules about keeping their world hidden from the human realm. And now, here he was, waiting like a giddy schoolboy for a woman who had no idea how much her life was about to change.

Keely wasn't just anybody though. She was his mate—his fated mate. The realization still hit him like a punch to the gut every time it crossed his mind. He could feel it in his very core, an unshakable pull toward her that defied logic, binding him to her in ways he couldn't fully explain. And yet, it felt oddly comforting, as if his entire being recognized she was finally here.

Cris ran a hand through his dark hair, staring out into the snowy expanse. The hum of the private jet approaching reached his ears, and his pulse quickened. It was too late to turn back now.

Moments later, the sleek jet came into view, its lights cutting through the falling snow as it descended toward the landing strip. Anticipation and excitement were swirled together with a bit of dread. What if she rejected him? Rejected her place here at the North Pole or with him? It had only been a few days, but the memory of their night together—her soft skin beneath his hands, the way she'd called his name—burned bright in his mind.

The jet landed smoothly, and the door opened, revealing Keely's silhouette. Even bundled up against the cold in her thick winter coat, she looked as breathtaking as ever, her cheeks flushed from the biting wind, her eyes wide with a mix of wonder and uncertainty. He had to remind himself to breathe as she stepped out onto the snowy ground, suitcase in hand. It was as if he could feel the connection between them snap into place the instant their eyes met across the snow-covered expanse, electric and undeniable.

Cris forced himself to keep his distance, maintain control, even though his instincts screamed at him to close the gap between them. This wasn't just about him and Keely. The future of Christmas was at stake, and bringing her here was already a gamble.

Scanning the landscape, Keely approached. "This is... incredible," she breathed, her voice barely audible over the wind. "I've never seen anything like this. It's like something out of a dream."

Cris allowed himself a small smile; he was reminded of why he had been so drawn to her in the first place. Keely had a way of seeing the world that was rare—unique—and that perspective might be the key to saving Christmas.

"Welcome to the North Pole," Cris said, his voice steady despite the storm of emotions raging inside him. "It's a little colder than what you're used to, but I promise you'll get used to it."

Keely met his gaze, and for a moment, neither of them moved. Cris's cock stiffened behind the fly of his jeans. The air between them was thick with the same magnetic pull that had been there since the moment they met. He fought off the urge to pull her into his arms and kiss her like he'd been dreaming of since the moment he left her bed.

But he couldn't. Not now. Not yet.

Keely finally broke the silence, her breath visible in the frigid air. "I have to admit, I'm still trying to wrap my head around all this. I mean, the North Pole? You weren't joking."

"I wasn't," Cris replied, his tone softening. "But there's a lot you still don't know, and I'll explain everything. For now, let's get out of this cold, and I'll show you around."

As they walked, Cris led her through the snowy landscape, the towering pines dusted in white like something out of a holiday postcard. They reached the massive, intricately carved wooden doors of the North Star Toys workshop. Cris hesitated for a moment before pushing them open, allowing the golden glow of the workshop to spill out into the night.

Keely's eyes widened as she stepped inside, and Cris couldn't help but watch her, captivated by the enchanted look that crossed her face. The workshop was bustling with activity—elves working at their stations—their pointed ears covered by their caps—as they created toys and gadgets with an energy that buzzed in the air. Cris had asked that at least for now they try to keep the magical elements out of sight. He wasn't sure Keely was ready for the whole truth. Even shifters sometimes had trouble believing in magic at first.

"This is incredible," she said, her voice filled with excitement. "I mean, I've worked in toy design for years, but this... this is like nothing I've ever seen. It's so... alive."

Cris smiled and felt tremendous pride in the workshop and her appreciation of it—seeing it through Keely's eyes reminded him of just how special it was. "Our goal here is to create toys that spark imagination, that bring joy and wonder to children all over the world. Your designs—those I've seen already—fit perfectly into that vision."

Keely's eyes flicked up to meet his with a hint of surprise. "You really think so?"

"I know so," Cris said, his voice low, more intimate than he had intended. He couldn't help it—being near her again, seeing the passion in her eyes, made it impossible to keep things strictly professional. "You have a gift, Keely. You see the world differently. And right now, that's exactly what we need... what I need."

Keely smiled softly, the tension between them crackling like a live wire. Cris struggled to keep his thoughts focused, but every time he looked at her, memories of their night together flooded his mind. Her laughter, her soft moans, the way she had fit so perfectly against him... She might be bundled up in winter clothing, but he knew what lay beneath.

Focus, Cris. This isn't the time.

He cleared his throat and gestured toward a series of workstations where elves were assembling prototype toys. "This is where the magic happens," he said, trying to steer the conversation back to business. "These are some of the best toy designers and crafters in the world."

Keely moved closer to one of the stations, her eyes lighting up as she studied the intricate mechanisms the elves were putting together. "This is amazing," she murmured, running her fingers over a half-assembled toy. "I've never seen craftsmanship like this."

Cris watched her, struck again by the ease with which she immersed herself in the world of toys. She was more than just a designer—she had a natural curiosity, a love for creation that was rare. As she examined the prototypes, collaboratively throwing out ideas and suggestions, Cris couldn't help but be impressed by her innovative thinking. She had a way of looking at things that made even the most seasoned toy makers stop and listen. They either nodded and agreed or when they didn't, entered into a spirited discussion. Cris could tell his people were already falling under her spell.

But more than that, he was drawn to her spirit, her energy. Every word she spoke, every laugh that escaped her lips, wrapped around his heart like a spell he couldn't break. And as much as he tried to push his feelings aside, to focus on the crisis they were facing, the attraction between them only grew stronger with each passing moment.

"You're full of surprises, Keely," Cris said softly, his eyes lingering on her as she turned to face him. "I knew you were talented, but this... you're exactly what we needed."

Keely met his gaze, her cheeks flushing slightly at his words. The air between them thickened, charged with an energy that neither of them could deny. Cris's heart pounded in his chest as he stepped closer, his dark eyes locked on hers, the magnetic pull drawing him in despite his best efforts to resist.

"I'm glad I came," Keely said, her voice barely above a whisper. "I'm not sure I understand why, though, as your people all seem so talented."

Cris swallowed, his pulse racing as he fought the urge to pull her into his arms. "You will, Keely. You will."

He knew that once she knew the truth—the whole truth—about this place, and about him, there would be no turning back.

For either of them.

They continued their tour of the workshop's production area before Cris showed her to her own workspace. They stowed her things, and he took her outside to show her the various support departments: a mess hall, a bakery, laundry, and the like.

Keely blushed as he showed her the bakery. She had mentioned during their one night together that she had indulged in more than one fantasy about going down on some 'hunky alpha male' in a bakery, knowing they might be caught at any minute. The scene had been in a book she'd once read. That small, uttered confession had been on his mind when he'd showed her the bakery, which at this time of day was deserted.

The deepening color in her cheeks indicated she remembered not only the fantasy she had shared with him but telling him about it. She turned to look at him. "The factory is amazing. It exceeds everything I've ever heard said about it."

Cris nodded. "We try to ensure our people have everything they need."

"It's almost like you don't want them to go anywhere."

"It isn't that," said Cris, shaking his head. "The plane makes routine flights south at least every other week; more often if needed, and employees fly at no cost to them. We just wanted to build something special—more of a community than just a place to work."

"I think you've done that. I would never have

imagined leaving Otter Cove, but this is just a kind of winter wonderland."

"Don't you think you'd miss the warm weather?"

Keely laughed. "Have you spent any time in Otter Cove? Trust me, warm weather isn't really much of an option. Some people like to take vacations in warm, sunny places with tropical breezes, but I really like the cold. It's kind of part of my nature."

"A snow bunny, perhaps?" he asked, teasingly.

"No. I like red meat. An arctic fox. Bunnies are cute; foxes are sexy."

That caught him by surprise. He thought he'd sensed she was a shifter. An arctic fox-shifter perhaps?

"Have I persuaded you to sign on as our new head toy designer?"

"I'm not sure I want to leave my home permanently, but Schultz Toys has been sold to Vanguard Holdings. If nothing else, I could come up and work with you and your people for the rest of the season."

"Done," he said, relieved. "I'm glad you've decided to at least come up and help us for the season. I have to tell you, ever since you told me about that scene from the book you read, I haven't been able to come in here without thinking about it."

Cris drew her close, backing her into a spot in the bakery where he knew they couldn't be easily seen, but one which would leave him where he could observe anyone approaching. It wasn't that they couldn't be seen if someone tried hard enough or walked in on them, but he suspected that would be part of the allure for Keely.

Looking up at him, she blushed again as she removed her coat and pulled her sweater over her head. Grinning mischievously and sensually, she placed her hands on his belt. "Funny, I was just thinking about that when we walked in here. Is there anything you'd like me to do for you, Sir?"

At that moment, he wasn't sure who'd set up who to fulfill her fantasy, and he didn't much care. All he knew was the woman whose bed he had shared and with whom he'd had the most glorious and prolific sex was standing right before him, just waiting for him to take charge.

He wasn't going to give her long to wait. "It would be hard for anyone to interrupt us without being noticed, especially if something had your full concentration."

She walked her fingers up his chest. "Do you have something you'd like me to focus on, Sir?" she teased.

"As a matter of fact, there are several things I can think of that need your attention, but one stands out in my mind right now."

"Would you like me to open your fly so it can stand out without restraint?"

"You know I would," he said, his voice dropping into a lower register. "I want you naked and on your knees, Keely. The memory of watching my cock slide in and out of your mouth crosses my mind more times a day than I thought would have been possible. But you need to know that's not why I brought you up here."

She pursed her lips in the most adorable pout. "It isn't? I can't tell you how disappointed I am."

He chuckled and reached out to cup her breast, flicking the stiffened nipple that was tenting the soft, thin lace bra she was wearing. "Let me amend that, it isn't the *only* reason I did it. Now, I believe I told you to get naked and on your knees. I want to fuck that sassy mouth of yours."

Smiling, Keely removed her clothes and then sank down onto her knees. She unbuckled his belt before unbuttoning his fly. Cris raised his eyebrow as he looked down at her, but he didn't give any sign that he objected. Emboldened, she helped his rigid cock escape to be admired in its raw, wonderful, and fully engorged state.

Keely licked her lips before parting them and taking him in, sucking gently at first and then harder as he let out a stifled moan. The fact that anyone could walk in and catch them or see them from outside only heightened the air of delicious and sultry danger.

Looking up at him, he watched as she began to suckle his cock in the most sensual way, paying homage to it in her own way. Perhaps she had missed him, too. His hand trailed down to caress her hair softly, guiding her head up and down his shaft.

Keely explored his pulsing length, running her tongue along the veining as her head bobbed up and down, taking more of him with each downward stroke. The sound of his cock sliding past her lips as she licked him, combined with his pleasured groans, filled the air. Keely swirled her tongue around the plum-shaped head of his cock, tasting him deeply before drawing back until only the tip was still in her mouth.

His fist curled into her hair, driving her head back down as he sought the velvety place at the back of her throat. Holding her in place, Cris began to thrust shallowly inside her mouth, gradually picking up speed and depth, taking control and not relinquishing it.

She seemed to find the taste of him intoxicating, allowing her to disregard the fear of whether they could be seen or not. He could smell the uptick in her arousal as she sucked while he fucked her mouth. He closed his eyes and moaned, remembering how good it had felt to be balls deep inside her.

The fabric of his jeans rubbed against the outside of her cheek as he grew larger in her mouth, twitching and swelling as he began to press even more deeply, pushing her to take all of him. He grunted and groaned, unable to hide his arousal and pleasure.

One hand held her head firmly in place, giving her

hair a small tug every time she tried to back off from him.

"God, yes," he murmured as he focused on his impending climax.

Harder and faster, he thrust in and out until finally he pushed her head down as he drove to the back of her throat, his cock shooting his seed down into her belly. Keely swallowed as fast as she could until he was done.

Cris released her hair, moving one hand down between them, stroking along her cheek and jawbone before finding its way to her chin. He grasped it between his thumb and forefinger, using it to pull her up from her knees for a deep kiss. Their tongues danced together hungrily as he pulled away from the kiss, panting heavily.

Cris stood close to Keely, the air between them buzzing with an almost unbearable tension. His gaze never left hers, drawn to the way her lips parted slightly as she looked up at him. The space around them felt small, intimate, and utterly charged with the magnetic pull that had been simmering between them since she stepped off the plane.

"God, I missed you," he confessed. "But as much as I'd just like to bend you over that worktable and fuck you hard before tossing you over my shoulder to carry you back to my bed, we do have work to do."

"Hmm... one fantasy to be replaced by another. Thank you, Sir."

He chuckled and leaned down to kiss her. "Get dressed," he ordered.

Keely took a small step back, reaching for her clothes. She got dressed, her eyes never leaving his. "You're so... intense," she whispered, her voice breathy and full of something that made his cock begin to tighten. "Ever since we met, it's like there's something... more. Something that shouldn't be, but feels like it's always been."

He nodded. She was right. There *was* something more—something neither of them could deny any longer. Cris took a step toward her, closing the distance between them, his heart pounding in his chest as his hand reached out, his fingers brushing lightly against her cheek. She leaned into his touch, her skin soft, warm, and alive beneath his palm. The connection between them flared like a flame, hotter, fiercer, pulling them both into its irresistible embrace.

"I don't know how this will all play out, but you need to know that I feel the same way," Cris murmured, his voice rough with the effort to contain himself. "But it's more than I've felt in... I can't explain it, Keely."

She smiled softly, her eyes searching his. Cris couldn't hold back any longer. He brought his lips crashing down on hers, claiming her in a kiss that was full of the longing and intensity that had been building between them from the moment they'd met. Keely responded instantly, her hands gripping the front of his shirt, pulling him closer as she kissed him back with just as much fervor.

Heat surged through Cris's veins as his hands slid around her waist, pulling her tightly against him. She melted into his embrace, her body pressing against his in a way that made his control slip even further. He wanted her—needed her—more than he could ever remember needing anyone. The fire between them roared to life as he deepened the kiss, his hands roaming, exploring, claiming every inch of her he could touch.

Keely moaned softly against his lips, her hands tangling in his hair, and Cris's heart raced with the knowledge that she felt it, too—this connection, this unstoppable force pulling them together. Every kiss, every touch, every ragged breath they shared only fueled the desire that burned between them.

He turned so her back pressed against the edge of the counter, the clutter of mixing bowls and baking trays forgotten as Cris's hands slid beneath her sweater, seeking the warmth of her skin. He felt her shiver under his touch, her breath hitching as he explored the soft curve of her waist, the intoxicating feel of her sending his senses spiraling. He wanted more—needed more of her, more of this, more of them.

Keely gasped as his lips trailed down her neck, her head falling back as she surrendered to the moment. Her fingers dug into his shoulders, and the heat of her breath against his skin was enough to drive him mad with want. Cris's mind raced, caught between the intensity of his desire and the knowledge that this—she—was unlike anything he had ever experienced.

But just as the moment deepened, the air filled with a sudden, deafening sound.

Alarms.

Cris froze, his senses jolting back to reality. The blaring sound cut through the haze of desire, reminding him of the responsibility he couldn't escape. He pulled back, his heart still racing, but the weight of his duties grounded him and reminded him that there was more at stake than just claiming Keely.

Keely looked up at him, her eyes wide with concern. "What... what is that?"

Cris clenched his jaw, struggling to tamp down the emotions swirling inside him. "It's the magic levels," he said, his voice tight with frustration.

"Magic levels?" she asked confused.

"Yes, I don't have time to explain. But they're important, and the alarm means they're dropping."

The bakery lights flickered, casting the room into a dim glow, and Cris's gut twisted with the reminder of the crisis they were still facing. He had let himself get swept up in the moment, in his growing feelings for Keely, but the reality of the situation came crashing back down.

Keely's hand found his, her touch grounding him, but also pulling him in two directions at once. "You need to go," she said softly, her voice full of understanding but also tinged with disappointment.

Cris nodded, torn. "I don't really have a choice, but I don't want to leave you... not right now," he admitted, his voice thick with the weight of his conflicted emotions. He cupped her face with his hand, his thumb brushing over her cheek, and for a moment, he wanted to forget everything—the alarms, the crisis, his responsibilities—and lose himself in her.

But he couldn't.

"I have to handle this," Cris said, forcing himself to step back, though every fiber of his being ached to stay with her. "I'll explain everything later, but right now... I've got to go."

Keely nodded, her gaze steady but filled with the same sense of loss he felt. "I understand," she whispered, though Cris could see the flicker of uncertainty in her eyes.

He leaned in, pressing a gentle kiss to her forehead, lingering just long enough to feel her sigh softly against him. "This isn't over," he promised, his voice low.

With a final look, Cris turned and ran toward the door. His responsibilities couldn't wait, not when the very magic that kept Christmas alive was slipping through their fingers. He could feel the weight of all that was at stake. But even as he rushed outside, the connection he felt with Keely burned bright, refusing to be extinguished.

As he hurried across the open space toward the heart of the North Pole's operations, Cris couldn't shake the growing sense of dread. Things were getting worse. The magic levels were dropping fast, and every moment they couldn't stop them increased the threat to Christmas itself. But as he ran, the snow crunching beneath his boots, one thought pulsed stronger than any other, and it wasn't concerning magic or Christmas or toys.

It was Keely.

No matter what was happening, no matter what challenges lay ahead, Cris knew one thing with absolute certainty—he wasn't letting her go. Now, he just had to figure out how to save Christmas... without losing her in the process.

CHAPTER
SIX
KEELY

Keely's office and workspace was off the main floor of the toy factory. She stared out the frosted window into the magical landscape of the North Star Toys facility. The snow glittered beneath the soft glow of the hanging lanterns outside, casting a surreal beauty over the scene. She'd barely caught her breath since arriving.

Cris had been called away almost immediately after their heated moment in the bakery. He'd apologized more than once, his intense gaze locking onto hers, promising he'd be back as soon as possible.

The sudden knock at her door startled her from her thoughts.

"Come in," Keely called, rising from the stool.

The door opened to reveal Holly, the petite, delicate girl who had introduced herself as one of Cris's chief toymakers. She was almost impossibly tiny, with bright, sparkling green eyes, a smattering of freckles across her nose, and a cheery smile that seemed to never leave her face. Today, she was bundled in a festive green and red coat with a furry collar.

"Hi, Keely!" Holly greeted with a bright, chipper tone as she stepped inside, a hint of snow still clinging to her coat. "I just wanted to let you know that the crisis has been averted. Cris managed to get everything stabilized, so everything is under control now. He's keeping an eye on things, but he should be back any time."

Keely breathed a sigh of relief. She hadn't been given many details about what was happening, but the way Cris had rushed off had made her worry. "Thank you, Holly. That's great news. Is he... is Cris okay?"

Holly nodded, her eyes softening. "He's fine, but unfortunately, he's still got a few things to take care of and then will be tied up in meetings and other stuff with the big boss. He won't be able to break away just yet."

Keely bit her lip, disappointment and something else—something she wasn't ready to admit—settling in her stomach. "That's okay. I understand. I'll just... dive into work."

Holly's smile widened, a sparkle of mischief in her eyes. "I'll bet you're like me, once you get started on something, it's easy to lose yourself in the magic of making toys. Knowing some kid will get their hands on it and have so much fun is a great feeling."

Keely nodded, offering her a small smile. "I do. It's so different here—and different in a good way. It's like nothing I've ever seen."

"Well, if you need anything," Holly said, "just ask. I'll be around. We elves are always—" She paused, her eyes widening in realization, her cheeks turning a slight shade of pink. "I mean... um, I'll be around, that's all."

Keely's brow furrowed, the word *elves* hanging in the air like an odd, unshakable mystery. "Did you just say elves?"

Holly's face turned even redder, and she laughed nervously, waving her hand. "Oh! Did I? Silly me! I just meant, you know, like... little helpers. It's just a joke we have around here. You know, Christmas spirit, Santa's helpers and all."

Keely narrowed her eyes slightly but didn't push it, a strange feeling nagging at the back of her mind. She'd noticed some peculiar things about the workshop and the way everything seemed to work in almost magical harmony. Still, she shrugged it off, deciding to focus on the work for now.

For the next few days, Keely threw herself into designing, sketching ideas, and experimenting with toy concepts. The workshop was an absolute wonderland, every corner brimming with whimsical tools and materials she had never dreamed existed. She found herself working closely with Tinker, a jovial, brilliant man with an odd habit of tinkering with gadgets that seemed far too advanced for a mere toy workshop.

Tinker was more than just a colleague—he had quickly become a sounding board for her most outlandish ideas, encouraging her creativity in ways no one ever had before. His enthusiasm was infectious, and Keely found herself growing more and more immersed in the work. But, even amidst the joy of creation, she couldn't help but notice the workshop's strange, almost unnatural efficiency. Toys were assembled at an impossibly fast pace, and the workers... well, they moved with an agility and speed that left her both impressed and puzzled.

One afternoon, as she'd watched a small group of workers putting the finishing touches on a set of interactive snow globes she had designed, something caught her eye. One of the workers—a quiet young man with dark hair tucked beneath a festive red cap—turned slightly as he reached for a tool. Keely's heart skipped a beat.

Peeking out from under his cap was what appeared to be the pointed tip of an ear.

Keely blinked, trying to process what she had seen. Her rational mind fought against the explanation that immediately surfaced, but the evidence was right there in front of her. Pointy ears. The kind of ears you only saw in storybooks or movies about... *elves*.

She'd watched the worker closely, but he seemed unaware of her scrutiny. As he moved about, his speed and precision were undeniable—unnatural, even. Keely's mind raced as she remembered it. Could it be that Holly hadn't been joking when she'd mentioned elves? Was this entire workshop staffed by...

"Keely, are you all right?" Tinker's voice broke through her thoughts, and she turned to find him watching her with a curious expression.

Keely quickly forced a smile. "Oh, I'm fine. Just... getting lost in all the amazing work here."

Tinker chuckled, nodding in agreement. "It's easy to do. We take pride in creating magic here, you know."

Magic. The word sent another shiver of curiosity down her spine. Was that really what was happening? Keely's rational side fought to make sense of it all, but the more time she spent here, the more things felt... impossible.

Later that evening, as she sat alone in her room, staring out into the snow-covered wonderland beyond the window, her thoughts circled back to Cris. She missed him. More than she wanted to admit. And she couldn't shake the feeling that there was something he wasn't telling her—something big. Her gaze flickered back to the sketches spread across her desk, but her mind was miles away.

She had been brought here for a reason, and somehow, it felt like more than just a consulting job. There was magic in the air—*real magic*—and Keely couldn't ignore it anymore. But what did it all mean? And more importantly, what role did she play in it?

As the night deepened, Keely's thoughts returned again and again to Cris. She needed answers. She needed him to tell her the truth. Because no matter how much her mind tried to rationalize it, she was starting to believe that this world was far more extraordinary than she could have ever imagined. And Cris Sutton was at the center of it all.

Tomorrow, she would find out. One way or another.

The following day, Keely resumed her work in the toy factory. Holly had popped in moments earlier, cheerily announcing that Cris had returned and would likely want to meet with Keely soon. Keely's heart had leapt at the news. As much as she wanted to focus on the work and the puzzle of this place, Cris had been a constant in her thoughts. Their connection, the pull between them—it was undeniable. She needed to see him, to talk to him, to understand what was really happening here.

Without giving herself too much time to second-guess, Keely threw on her coat and headed out into the icy afternoon, her breath coming out in soft puffs as she made her way through the snowy wonderland of the North Pole. The cold nipped at her cheeks, but it did little to deter her.

The snow crunched beneath her boots as she wandered toward the small field near the company's airstrip, a place she had found herself gravitating toward whenever she needed a moment to think.

It was still early in the afternoon, and the world around her was blanketed in a fresh layer of powdery snow, undisturbed by footprints or activity. The field was wide open, with the private jet she had arrived in parked at the far edge, its metallic surface gleaming in the soft light. The quiet serenity of the place always brought her a sense of peace, but today, there was an electric charge in the air—something she couldn't quite place.

As she drew closer to the field, a sudden movement caught her eye. She stopped, squinting through the soft snowfall to focus on what appeared to be a large, dark figure at the far end of the field, just beyond the plane.

Keely blinked, unsure of what she was seeing. It was a moose—a massive, majestic creature with towering antlers, like a crown, that seemed to reach toward the sky. But as far as she knew, there were no moose indigenous to the North Pole, and yet there it was. Its dark coat stood out sharply against the snowy backdrop, and for a moment, Keely's breath caught in her throat at the sight of it.

But then, something extraordinary happened.

The moose—this enormous, grounded animal—began to move in ways that defied logic. With a graceful bound, it lifted its heavy body into the air, as if the snow beneath its hooves had turned weightless. Keely's eyes widened as she watched the moose leap into the air, its legs outstretched, and then—it happened again. The moose, impossibly large, seemed to cavort through the field as though gravity had simply lost its grip on it.

It twirled midair with a surprising elegance, its antlers slicing through the air in slow motion, almost as if the world had tilted into a dream. Keely gasped, watching as it bounded in great, joyful leaps, each one higher than the last, until it was practically dancing across the field, the snow swirling beneath it.

She stood frozen in place, captivated by the sight, her rational mind struggling to comprehend what was happening. *Moose don't fly*—that was her first thought, but here it was, defying every law of nature as it pranced and twirled in midair, moving with a fluid grace that didn't belong to a creature of its size.

It circled the company plane once, twice, leaping higher each time, before landing softly back in the snow with barely a sound. For a moment, it stood still, its dark eyes glistening in the afternoon light, watching her with an intelligence that seemed far beyond that of a simple animal.

Keely's heart pounded in her chest as she took a hesitant step forward, her breath catching in her throat. Was this some kind of trick? An illusion? She shivered, not from the cold but from the unsettling feeling that her world was once again turning upside down, and the truth—whatever it was—was closer than ever to being revealed.

And then, without warning, a localized swirl of snow whipped up around the moose, forming a small cyclone that spiraled upward, circling the massive animal like a vortex. The wind picked up, though it didn't seem to touch the rest of the landscape—it was concentrated solely around the moose.

Keely's heart pounded in her chest as she watched, frozen in place, her wide eyes locked on the swirling storm. Snow flew wildly in the air, but despite the chaos, the moose remained eerily calm, as though the storm was a part of it.

Suddenly, the snowstorm stilled, and with one final gust, the wind fell away completely. Keely blinked, her breath catching in her throat.

The moose was gone. Standing in its place, his breath heavy, his dark hair tousled by the wind, was Cris. He was naked, his broad, muscular frame bathed in the soft glow of the sun, his skin flushed from the cold but unaffected by it. She'd been right; he was a shifter.

Cris's eyes caught hers, and for a split second, they both froze, the air between them thick with shock and something deeper, something raw. His dark eyes, full of intensity, locked onto hers, and Keely's heart thudded painfully in her chest.

She had just witnessed the impossible. Keely had been pretty sure Cris was a shifter, just not what kind. Now she knew he was a moose shifter, and not just any moose shifter, but one that could fly. Everyone at North Star Toys talked about magic and how it infused everything, and now she knew that the magic was real and was pretty sure that Cris's boss was a jolly old fat man in a red suit.

It was as if everything began to crowd in on her. She could feel herself going weak in the knees. The last thing she saw as she slowly slid to the ground was Cris's expression shifting from shock to concern, his lips parting as if to call her name.

The snow cushioned her fall, and as the world faded around her, the only thing that remained in her mind was the image of Cris—and the moose—before it all slipped away into darkness.

CHAPTER
SEVEN
CRIS

Cris's heart was heavy as the North Star jet cut through the clear sky, heading back to the North Pole. The weight of the betrayal he'd just uncovered hung over him like a cloud he couldn't shake. His mind churned with anger and frustration, the irrefutable truth of Jack's—no... he could never think of him as Jack again. He was Frost, and his treachery played over and over in Cris's head.

Vanguard Holdings. It all made sense now—Frost had orchestrated everything. He had created that soulless corporation to buy out the best toy companies, turning them into money-making machines devoid of magic, innovation, or wonder. Cris gritted his teeth, the familiar swell of rage bubbling inside him. Frost had betrayed them all, all for the sake of power and wealth. But worse than that, Frost's plan was not only to make himself rich, but to destroy the heart of Christmas itself.

The North Pole had been Cris's sanctuary for so long. He'd been entrusted with one of Santa's most powerful gifts: the ability to fly in his shifted form, allowing him to harness magic and protect the North Pole. Cris had always believed in what they did—keeping the magic of Christmas alive for children and others who believed around the world. Now, the discovery that Frost—someone he had once considered both a friend and ally—was the mastermind behind all that had been happening tore at his very core.

As the plane began its descent, the familiar snowy landscape of the North Pole coming into view, Cris's anger intensified. He needed to shake this off before he returned to the workshop. He couldn't let the others see the storm brewing inside him. Not now. Not when everything was so precariously balanced.

The jet touched down on the snow-covered runway with a soft thud, the magic of the North Pole making the landing feel smooth and gentle despite the turbulence inside his heart. As the plane taxied to a stop, Cris rose from his seat and headed straight for the door. He needed air. He needed freedom.

The cold hit him the moment he stepped outside, but it did little to quell the fire burning inside. Without a second thought, he made his way into the open field by the airstrip, his boots crunching through the snow. The stillness of the place, the untouched beauty of the snowy landscape, was a stark contrast to the turmoil within him.

He knew what he needed to do.

Closing his eyes and called forth his moose. The familiar warmth spread through his body, the shift beginning as the air around him crackled with energy. His muscles rippled, the snow swirling up around him as his form shifted from human to something much larger, much more powerful. In a matter of moments, Cris stood as a massive moose, his antlers stretching high into the night sky, his dark eyes glistening as the transformation completed.

With a snort, he shook his large head, tossing the snow from his antlers as he began to move. Slowly at first, his powerful legs carrying him across the snowy field, the weight of his thoughts slowly lifting with each step. The freedom of his moose form was intoxicating, a wildness that let him escape the burden of leadership, of responsibility.

As he began to run, his massive hooves thundering across the snow, he felt the weight of his anger and guilt start to slip away. The wind whipped through his fur, and with a leap, he invoked the special magic Santa had granted him—the ability to dance in the air, to fly for short bursts. The snow swirled beneath him as he bounded up, his massive body soaring into the sky with an elegance that defied his size.

He couldn't fly for long—not like the reindeer—but in these short, exhilarating bursts, he felt weightless, as if he could leave everything behind. The magic of the North Pole surged through him, lifting him higher, the snow swirling in a beautiful, spiraling dance around him. He twirled and cavorted in the sky, feeling the joy and freedom that came with his moose form. For a few moments, there was no betrayal, no anger—only the pure magic of the air and the snow.

He landed gracefully, the snow cushioning his landing, and stood there for a moment, panting softly as the energy of his flight dissipated. The rage that had gnawed at him earlier felt distant now, like a shadow he had left behind in the sky.

But as he began to shift back, something caught his eye.

Cris froze mid-transformation, halfway between moose and man, as he spotted a figure standing at the edge of the field. His heart dropped. His eyes locked with hers as he finished his shift.

Keely was standing there, her eyes wide, her breath coming out in visible puffs in the cold air. Her expression was a mixture of shock and disbelief, her body frozen as if she couldn't quite process what she had just seen. And then she crumpled to the ground.

MERRY CRIS MOOSE

∼

Cris paced outside the infirmary, grateful to Holly for having brought him so clothes so he could get redressed. His breath coming in ragged bursts that had little to do with the cold air of the North Pole. His boots crunched against the snow-dusted walkway, the sound steady but doing nothing to calm the storm raging inside him. The tension gnawed at his gut—Keely had seen everything. She had witnessed him flying. And now, she was lying unconscious inside, the shock of it all too much for her.

He replayed the scene over and over in his mind, her wide eyes locked on him as she watched him shift from moose back into man, the disbelief and confusion that had clouded her face before she collapsed into the snow. Cris had rushed to her side, scooping her up in his arms, his heart pounding with fear and guilt. What had he done? He had tried to protect her until he thought she was ready, but now everything was out in the open. Maybe it was for the best.

He leaned against the stone wall, staring out at the snowy expanse of the North Pole. His mind was a whirlwind of conflicting emotions. His duty to protect the secrecy and security of this magical place clashed violently with the undeniable pull he felt toward Keely. He had sworn to protect this place, to keep its secrets from the human world, and yet here he was, breaking that oath for a woman who had somehow captured his heart. Granted she was shifter, but still...

How could he let her into this world? How could he not?

The door to the infirmary creaked open, and Holly stepped out, her small frame bundled up in a thick, festive coat, her green eyes shining with concern. "She's awake," Holly said gently. "You should go to her."

Cris's heart leapt at the words, but the weight of guilt and uncertainty kept his feet rooted to the ground. "How is she?"

Holly gave him a soft smile, her cheeks flushed pink from the cold. "Confused, but... she seems okay. More than okay, really."

Cris's brow furrowed. He had expected Keely to be shaken, maybe even terrified. She was bright; she'd seen him fly. It wouldn't take much for her to put the pieces together. He could well imagine how it must feel to see the impossible—a world she had perhaps dreamed about but had never seen.

"She's not... scared?" he asked.

Holly shook her head, her smile widening slightly. "More like... intrigued. I think you'll be surprised."

With a deep breath, Cris nodded and forced himself to walk through the door, his heart hammering in his chest. He steeled himself for the conversation ahead, not knowing how he would explain everything to her, but he knew one thing for sure—he couldn't lie to her anymore. Whatever questions she asked, he would answer.

The moment he stepped into the room, his eyes landed on Keely, sitting up in the bed. Her cheeks were still flushed, but her wide eyes were bright with a mix of curiosity and something else... something that looked an awful lot like excitement. When she saw him, her lips curved into a soft smile.

"Hey," she said, her voice light but a little uncertain. "So... you can fly? Cool. I guess we need to talk."

Cris swallowed hard and walked over to her, pulling up a chair beside the bed. He rubbed the back of his neck, unsure of how to start. "Keely, I—" He stopped, his voice heavy with guilt. "I'm sorry. You weren't supposed to see that. I wanted to explain it all to you... but not like this."

She tilted her head, a glimmer of amusement in her eyes. "You mean, you weren't going to tell me you can fly?"

Cris shrugged, unsure of how to proceed with everything he needed to say. "Yes. I can fly. It was a gift from..."

"Santa?" she supplied.

He grinned sheepishly. "Yes, a gift from Santa." He ran a hand through his hair, his heart pounding. "My guess is you've figured out that there's real magic here. Santa, elves, the whole spirit of Christmas."

She nodded. "Scrooge gets ghosts and a nightmare. I get a flying moose. I think I like mine better."

He shook his head at her almost childlike wonder. He blinked, caught off guard by not only her acceptance, but also her enthusiasm. "So you believe?"

Keely let out a breathless laugh, shaking her head in disbelief but clearly delighted. "I saw you fly with my own eyes. I saw a moose fly. You know your kind isn't known for their grace of movement, but when you were up there, it was almost like you were dancing. It was really beautiful—powerful, but beautiful. As for believing the rest of it—Santa, elves—I *want* to believe it. I can't tell you how much I've always wanted to believe, and now I can."

Cris stared at her, completely stunned. He had been prepared for anger, for fear, for rejection, for anything but this. He had never imagined she would embrace it so easily, so openly. "You're not... freaked out?"

Keely smiled, her eyes bright with excitement. "Are you kidding? I'm thrilled. I mean, it's a lot to take in, but... I've always loved Christmas. I've always believed in the magic of it, even if I thought it was just a story. And now... I get to be part of it."

Cris felt a wave of relief wash over him. Keely wasn't going to run away. She wasn't scared. She was here, with him, and she was accepting everything about his world with an open heart and open arms.

But before he could respond, Keely's brow furrowed as she looked at him more seriously. "So, what's going on? I've heard people whispering about having to save or to protect Christmas. From what?"

Cris snorted. "Not just what, but who. We keep a sharp eye on people's belief in the magic of Christmas. We've been monitoring it pretty closely and have figured out it is fading. It's one of the reasons why I brought you here—your ideas, your toys, I think they have the potential to reignite children's belief in Christmas. Tinker and everyone else agrees. But what I've discovered is that the magic isn't just fading, someone has been actively trying to steal the remaining magic."

Keely's eyes widened. "Who?"

"Frost," Cris said, his voice bitter.

"As in Jack Frost?"

"He used to be one of us," Cris explained, nodding. "He created a company called Vanguard Holdings..."

"Vanguard? That's who bought Schultz Toys."

"I know. He's been buying out innovative toy companies, tying up the best designers so that they either worked for him or were bound by non-competition agreements. Then he turned the companies he bought into profit-driven machines. He's taking the magic out of toys, turning them into something cold and empty. And if he succeeds... Christmas as we know it will disappear."

Keely's mouth dropped open in shock, but then her eyes narrowed. "So that's why you brought me here. You think my designs can help."

Cris nodded. "I do. Your toys, the way they spark imagination—they're what we need to fight back. If we can reignite the magic in children's hearts, we can stop Frost."

For a moment, Keely was silent, clearly processing everything. Then, slowly, a grin spread across her face. "Well, if that's what we need to do, I have a few ideas."

Cris chuckled, feeling his tension ease as he watched her excitement. Despite everything, Keely's mind was already spinning with ideas, and for the first time in days, he felt a glimmer of hope. He was beginning to believe they might just be able to stop Frost.

But just as the warmth between them began to settle, a sharp, sudden tremor rocked the room, followed by a loud crack that echoed through the walls. Cris shot to his feet.

"What the hell was that?" asked Keely. "Oh wait, can I say hell?"

Criss nodded. "It's the magical barrier around the North Pole—it sounds like it's weakening. It has to be Frost."

Before he could say more, Holly burst into the room, her face pale with fear. "Cris, it's Frost! He's here. He's attacking the North Pole, and he's not alone."

Cris could feel his blood turn to ice as the gravity of the situation slammed into him. Frost was making his move. He was making a direct attack. He was here to steal the remaining magic, and he wouldn't stop until he'd drained every last bit of Christmas spirit from the North Pole.

Cris turned to Keely, his eyes full of urgency. "Stay here. You'll be safe."

But Keely shook her head as she tossed the bedding aside. "No way. I'm not sitting this out. I'm coming with you."

Cris opened his mouth to argue, but there was no time. The sound of another explosion ripped through the air, and he knew they had to move fast. He grabbed Keely's hand, his heart pounding with the knowledge that everything—Christmas, their world, and whatever was blossoming between them—was hanging by a thread.

CHAPTER
EIGHT
KEELY

Keely stood in the middle of the snow-covered field, her breath coming in ragged bursts as she stared at the chaos unfolding around her. The once peaceful North Pole had turned into a battleground. Her heart raced as she watched in awe and horror, her mind barely able to process what was happening. Magical beings she had never imagined were really true now stood before her, defending the very essence of Christmas from an unimaginable enemy.

Cris, in his massive moose form, charged through the snow, his antlers gleaming as he plowed into Frost's minions—hulking creatures that looked like twisted, evil versions of the abominable snowman she remembered from an old holiday special. Except these monsters weren't cartoonish. They were terrifying.

Their fur was matted and dark, their eyes glowing with an eerie blue light, and when they opened their mouths, they revealed jagged, razor-sharp teeth that seemed to sparkle with the promise of violence. Even worse, they wielded bows, shooting arrows made of ice that exploded into dangerous shards as they neared their targets.

Every time one of those arrows landed, it shattered with a loud crack, sending jagged pieces of ice in every direction. Cris dodged them with impressive agility for his size, but Keely could feel the strain as he fought and the toll it was taking on him. She had never felt more helpless—or more out of place—in her life.

There was no time for hesitation or second-guessing. She had chosen to stay, and now, standing among elves and reindeer shifters, she needed to find a way to contribute. Cris had told her to stay safe, but Keely was committed to helping in whatever way she could. She refused to be a bystander.

Holly appeared by her side, her usually bright eyes now sharp with focus on the job at hand. The small elf moved with surprising speed and grace, clutching a glowing staff in her hand. "Keely! We have to protect the workshop—the letters to Santa!" Holly shouted over the noise of the battle, pointing toward the large workshop behind them. "If Frost gets his hands on the children's letters, it could weaken everything past the point we can save it."

Keely's heart skipped a beat. The letters. She had seen how important they were—how they helped fuel the spirit that made everything possible here. If they were destroyed, the damage could be irreversible.

"I'm with you!" Keely replied, her voice strong despite the fear twisting in her gut. She darted after Holly, her boots slipping slightly on the ice as they ran toward the workshop. Arrows of ice whizzed past them, and one exploded just a few feet away, sending shards scattering. Keely ducked, narrowly avoiding the sharp pieces, her pulse racing.

As they reached the workshop, they were met by Tinker, who was frantically working on reinforcing the building's magical defenses. The usually jovial elf was all business now, his hands moving with precise efficiency as he tinkered with a glowing mechanism by the front door. "This isn't going to hold for long," Tinker warned, his voice tight with worry. "Frost's magic is too strong. We need to secure those letters, fast."

Keely's mind raced. She wasn't magical like the others, but she was inventive. If there was one thing she knew how to do, it was think outside the box.

An idea began to form. "Wait," she said, her voice hurried. "The toy designs we've been working on—some of the prototypes. We could use them! They're interactive, right? Designed to inspire creativity. What if we modified them to create distractions? Or defenses?"

Tinker's eyes lit up. "That might just work," he said nodding.

Keely didn't hesitate. She sprinted toward one of the workstations inside the workshop, where a few of her prototypes were still in development. Her fingers moved quickly, grabbing a handful of toys—a flying dragon that shot out bubbles, an enchanted snow globe that created mini-avalanches, and a wind-up bear that played holiday tunes. Working together, she, Holly and Tinker were able to modify them, tweaking the enchantments just enough to enhance their capabilities.

"These won't hold off Frost's minions for long," Tinker warned as they finished setting up the makeshift defenses. "But they'll buy us some time."

"That's all we need," Keely replied, her voice steady with newfound confidence.

They hurried outside, just as another wave of Frost's icy minions advanced toward the workshop. Keely's heart pounded in her chest, but there was no time to think about fear. She launched the flying dragon into the air, its wings beating rapidly as it soared above the battlefield, releasing a barrage of shimmering bubbles. The bubbles, however, weren't just for show. They expanded in size, creating barriers that blocked the incoming ice arrows, causing them to explode harmlessly in midair.

Holly waved her glowing staff, sending a wave of magic through the snow globe. Suddenly, mini avalanches formed around the feet of Frost's minions, tripping them up as they tried to advance. Some of them snarled in frustration as they tumbled to the ground, their icy bows shattering upon impact.

The wind-up bear toddled forward, playing a cheery holiday tune that sounded almost absurd amidst the chaos of battle, but the enchantment Tinker had added caused the tune to disrupt the flow of magic in the air. The creatures faltered, their connection to Frost's magic weakening just enough to give Cris and the other defenders an edge.

Keely's breath came in short gasps as she watched her creations in action, her pulse racing with a mix of excitement and fear. For the first time since the battle had started, she felt like she was making a real difference. She glanced toward Cris, who had shifted back into his human form, donned a red Santa suit and was now fighting hand-to-hand with one of the larger creatures. His eyes caught hers for a brief moment, and there was a flicker of pride in his gaze—he saw what she had done.

But the battle was far from over.

A deep, bone-chilling cold swept through the air, and Keely's gaze snapped to the far edge of the battlefield, where a figure in shimmering, ice-covered armor stepped forward.

Frost.

His presence alone sent a shiver of fear down Keely's spine. His cold blue eyes glowed with malice, and with a single flick of his wrist, a massive wall of ice erupted from the ground, barreling toward the defenders. Cris barely had time to dodge out of the way, but others weren't as lucky—some of the reindeer shifters were knocked back, their forms crumpling in the snow.

Frost's cold, hollow laugh echoed through the air as he strode forward, his minions rallying around him. "You think you can stop me with toys and trinkets?" he sneered, his voice as cold as the air itself. "Christmas is mine to control now."

Keely's heart sank, but she refused to give in to fear. She glanced toward Holly, Tinker, and Cris, knowing that they were depending on her. She had to think, had to find a way to outsmart Frost before it was too late.

Her gaze flickered toward the workshop, and an idea began to take shape.

"Holly," she whispered urgently, "I need your help."

Together, she, Holly and Tinker raced back inside, Keely's mind spinning with possibilities. If they could combine magic with the power of imagination, if they could create something that even Frost wouldn't see coming...

"We have to act fast," Holly said urgently.

Tinker nodded. "We were starting to beat them back, but now that Frost is here..."

As they worked, Keely could feel the tension all around her, but she also felt surrounded by the magic and creativity of the workshop, she knew one thing for certain: she belonged here. She might not be magical —although shifting was a kind of magic—but maybe she and the others could turn the tide on Frost.

She would do whatever it took to protect this place, to protect Christmas, and to protect Cris. Whatever Frost was going to throw at them, Keely and the others were ready. The letters to Santa were safe, stowed safely away in a hidden vault beneath the workshop, but they were far from out of danger. Frost's icy minions still surrounded the North Pole, and outside, the battle raged on. They had to find another way to fight back—and fast.

Tinker was already rifling through the collection of half-built toys when Keely's eyes landed on one of the newer prototypes she'd been working on—a laser light projector designed to create dazzling holiday displays. The idea was simple: children could program the toy to project snowflakes, Christmas trees, or even dancing reindeer onto walls or ceilings, creating their own light shows. But it was more than just a toy—the light it emitted was a powerful laser. They'd been working to make it safe enough for kids, but right now, that wasn't of paramount importance.

"We can use this," she said, grabbing the laser projector from the workbench.

Tinker turned to her, his brow furrowing. "That's a light projector, Keely, not a weapon, and we still haven't worked out the kinks."

"Maybe not for kids, but for what we need it for, it's just fine," Keely said as her fingers flew over the controls, adjusting the settings as she talked. "It's a laser—a light or heat laser. What's the best thing to kill ice and snow with?"

Tinker nodded. "You just might be on to something. If we can amplify it enough to disrupt Frost's dark magic and his minions, we can use it to hit his forces where it hurts."

Holly grinned. "That might actually work. We'd need to boost the energy output, though. And aim it. Oooh, I've got an idea," she said rushing over with a set of tools—the likes of which Keely had never seen before.

Holly began tweaking the projector's inner workings, her fingers moving with precision and speed as she rewired the device. "If we can reconfigure the power source to tap into the workshop's main power grid, we can give it enough juice to take down those ice monsters."

Keely worked alongside her, adjusting the output settings and recalibrating the targeting mechanism. Sweat trickled down her brow as she focused, her mind racing. She pushed everything else aside—the sounds of the battle, Cris's safety, all of it—zeroing in on the task at hand.

"There," Holly said finally, standing back and wiping her hands on her coat. "It's ready. We've increased the output tenfold. We should be able to fire it like a cannon."

Keely gripped the newly modified laser projector, feeling the hum of magic and power coursing through it. "Let's test it."

Together, the three of them moved outside, positioning the projector near the entrance of the workshop. Keely adjusted the targeting mechanism, her hands trembling slightly as she lined up the shot. Further afield, Cris and the other defenders were still battling Frost's forces—hulking abominable snowmen that were hurling shards of ice in every direction.

Keely took a deep breath and activated the projector.

A beam of pure, shimmering light shot out from the device, cutting through the snow-filled air like a hot knife through butter. The beam struck one of Frost's minions directly in the chest, and the creature let out a guttural roar as the light engulfed it. The ice creature was disintegrated in a matter of seconds, leaving nothing but a puff of mist behind.

"It works!" Keely shouted, adrenaline surging through her. She quickly recalibrated the projector, aiming it at another approaching creature. This time, when she fired, the beam sliced through not one, but two of the monsters, dissolving them into nothingness.

Tinker cheered beside her. "You did it!"

But Keely didn't have time to celebrate. More of Frost's forces were closing in. Cris closed the distance between them and kissed her. "You are amazing."

Grabbing the gun, he repositioned the projector, his hands flying over the controls as he fired shot after shot. Each beam of light tore through the icy minions with precision, turning them to mist before they could reach the workshop.

As he continued to fire, her eyes flickered toward Cris. His movements were quick, fluid, and powerful—there was something undeniably captivating about watching him fight. The way his muscles flexed, the raw determination in his eyes... her breath caught in her throat.

She realized she was in love with him. Completely, hopelessly in love.

Cris was more than just Santa's Chief of Staff, more than a moose-shifter with a protective streak. He was the one who had shown her the magic of this place, the one who had believed in her ideas and trusted her to help save Christmas. And now, seeing him fight so fiercely to protect everything they both cared about, she felt drawn to him with an emotion that was undeniable. Could they be *fated mates?*

Her mind swirled with questions, but before she could dwell on them, another ice arrow whizzed past, shattering against the side of the workshop. Keely snapped back to reality, focusing once again on the battle. Cris aimed the projector at the source of the arrow and fired, obliterating another of Frost's minions in a burst of light.

The tide of the battle was turning. The defenders were rallying, pushing back against Frost's forces with renewed strength. Cris, Holly, Tinker, and the others fought fiercely, and with the help of the laser cannon, they began to drive the icy creatures back toward the edge of the battlefield.

Finally, after what felt like hours of fighting, the last of Frost's minions crumbled under the force of the defenders' combined efforts. The battlefield grew quiet, save for the howling wind and the soft crunch of snow beneath their feet.

Cris lowered the projector. Keely's heart was still pounding, but the adrenaline was beginning to fade, leaving her exhausted but relieved. They had done it—they had held off Frost's attack. For now, at least, the North Pole was safe.

Cris appeared at her side, his breath coming in short gasps, his dark eyes searching hers. "Are you okay?" he asked, his voice rough but full of concern.

Keely nodded, her heart fluttering at the intensity of his gaze. "I'm fine. Thanks to this." She gestured toward the projector, giving him a small, tired smile. "And thanks to you."

Cris's expression softened, and he reached out, brushing a stray lock of hair from her face. The simple touch sent a jolt of warmth through her, a reminder of the connection between them that had only grown stronger since they'd met.

"We couldn't have done this without you," Cris said softly, his voice low and full of meaning

Keely's breath hitched, her chest tightening with emotion. The weight of the battle, the magic, the undeniable bond between them—it was all too much to ignore. She looked up at him, her heart pounding, her voice barely a whisper.

"I don't know what happens next," she said, her eyes locking onto his, "but I know that I don't want to lose this. I don't want to lose you."

Cris's gaze darkened, and the air between them crackled with unspoken desire. He stepped closer, his hand lingering on her cheek as his thumb brushed over her skin. "You won't lose me, Keely," he whispered, his voice rough with emotion. "You're my fated mate. I love you. I knew it the moment I met you."

Keely's heart soared, her fears melting away in the warmth of his words. There it was—confirmation of the bond she had felt growing between them from the start. *Fated mates.* It was real. "I love you, too," she said softly.

And then, before she could say more, Cris leaned in, his lips brushing against hers, soft at first, then deepening as the heat between them flared to life. Keely melted into the kiss, her arms wrapping around his neck as she let herself fall completely into the moment.

In that kiss, there was no battle, no danger—only them. Only the magic that had brought them together.

CHAPTER
NINE
CRIS

Cris stood in the North Pole's command center, the screens in front of him glowing with activity as his eyes darted between the figures shown. The miniature figures of reindeer shifters and elves moved swiftly, coordinating their defenses against Frost's latest attack. His brow furrowed with concentration as he strategized, giving rapid orders to the team. Every instinct told him this was far from over—Frost was still out there, plotting his next move, and the North Pole's defenses had to be stronger than ever.

But even as he focused on the task at hand, Cris couldn't shake the gnawing anxiety that had taken root inside him. His mind kept drifting back to Keely. She had thrown herself into the battle without hesitation, her creativity and courage turning the tide in their favor. He admired her for it, loved her even more for the way she embraced this magical world so completely.

She was his fated mate; he'd accepted it. What he hadn't counted on was the way she had so completely captured his heart. She was the woman he had been waiting for all his life. There were times he woke up early in the morning just so he could watch her sleeping in his bed. There was something profoundly satisfying about that. The bond between them was undeniable, like gravity pulling him toward her every time they were near. And when they kissed, everything else faded away and Cris felt that deep connection solidify. She was his, and he was hers.

As much as he loved her, as much as he wanted her by his side, Cris couldn't ignore the fact that Keely was in danger—and it was because of him. Frost wasn't going to stop until he had drained every last drop of Christmas magic from the North Pole, and Keely, with her creative spark and boundless determination, was now part of the fight. He had brought her into this world, into the heart of a war she hadn't asked for.

He had put her in harm's way—his fated mate, the woman he was supposed to protect above all others. He should have kept her out of this, should have found another way to stop Frost without dragging her into the conflict. But instead, he had brought her here, to the front lines of a battle that was growing more dangerous by the hour.

And it wasn't just the physical danger that worried him. Frost was more than just a foe—they had once been allies. Friends, even. Cris had confided in Frost about the pressures of being Santa's Chief of Staff, the constant weight of responsibility that came with ensuring Christmas ran smoothly year after year. And in a moment of vulnerability, Cris had shared his plans to bring Keely to the North Pole, believing Frost to be someone he could trust.

Now, that trust felt like a cruel joke.

How could I have been so blind?

Had Frost used Cris's own words to formulate his plans, knowing exactly how to exploit his weaknesses? The thought made his stomach turn.

A soft knock on the door pulled him from his dark thoughts, and Cris looked up to see Keely standing in the doorway. She looked different now—stronger and more confident, but there was still a softness in her eyes when she looked at him, a warmth that settled the storm inside him, if only for a moment.

"Hey," she said softly, stepping into the room. "I thought I'd find you here. Everything okay?"

Cris nodded, though his heart was far from settled. "Yeah. Just making sure the defenses are holding." He gestured to the glowing snow globe in front of him, where tiny figures moved in and out of view. "Frost's forces are regrouping. We're preparing for another attack."

Keely's eyes flicked toward the snow globe, her brow furrowing with concern. "You think he'll come back sooner rather than later?"

Cris sighed, running a hand through his hair. "We're all working against the same clock. Frost isn't done yet. He wants to destroy Christmas, and he won't stop until he does. We've bought ourselves some time, but not much."

Keely moved closer, her presence a comforting warmth in the cold room. "We'll stop him, Cris. We will."

Her words were strong, confident, but Cris could see the small amount of doubt that lingered in her eyes. She was brave, no doubt about that, but she had never faced an enemy like Frost before. And that was what scared him the most—he had brought her into a world of magic and danger, and now he wasn't sure if he could protect her from what was coming.

Cris turned toward her, his eyes locking onto hers. "Keely, I need you to know something." His voice was low, heavy with emotion. "When I brought you here, I didn't think it would get this dangerous. I didn't know Frost was behind all of this. And now... I'm worried about what could happen to you."

Keely's eyes softened as she reached out, placing her hand on his arm. "Cris, I would have chosen to come even if I'd known everything. My place is here with you. I'm a part of this, whether you like it or not."

Cris shook his head, his heart aching. "Don't you get it? You're my fated mate, Keely. I'm supposed to protect you, to keep you safe. But I feel like I've put you in harm's way instead."

Keely stepped closer, her hand sliding up to cup his cheek, her touch gentle and grounding. "You didn't put me in danger, Cris. Frost did. And I'm not some helpless human or little fox shifter who needs to be shielded. I'm your fated mate, remember? Like it or not, we're in this together."

The raw intensity of her words cut through his guilt. She was right—they were fated mates. They were supposed to be stronger together than apart. But still, the fear lingered, the fear of losing her, of failing to protect the person who meant more to him than anything else.

"You're stronger than I could've ever imagined," he whispered, his voice thick with emotion. "But that doesn't stop me from worrying."

Keely smiled softly, her thumb brushing over his cheek. "I worry about you, too, you know. You've been carrying the weight of the North Pole on your shoulders for years, and now you're facing Frost—a man you trusted, a man you once called friend. He betrayed you. He betrayed all of you."

Her words sent a shot of warmth spreading

through his system that dulled the edge of his concern. He leaned into her touch, closing his eyes for a moment as he allowed himself to simply feel her, to let her presence soothe the turmoil inside him.

"I love you, Keely," he murmured.

Keely smiled. "I know. I love you, too," she whispered.

For a moment, the world outside disappeared—the battle, the danger, all of it faded away, leaving just the two of them in that quiet, intimate space. Cris leaned down, capturing her lips in a kiss that was filled with all the love and longing he had never even allowed himself to imagine. Keely wrapped her arms around his neck as she snuggled against him, her warmth melting the coldness inside him.

The kiss deepened, their connection flaring to life with a heat that was undeniable. Cris's hands slid around her waist, pulling her closer as he lost himself in the feel of her, the taste of her. It was as though everything he had ever wanted, everything he had ever needed, was right there in his arms.

But even as the heat between them built, a small voice in the back of Cris's mind reminded him of the danger still looming outside. Frost was still out there, still planning his next move, and the North Pole wasn't safe yet.

Reluctantly, Cris pulled back, his breath ragged as he rested his forehead against hers. "We'll get through this," he whispered, his voice rough with emotion. "I promise."

Keely smiled up at him, her eyes full of understanding and acceptance. "I know we will."

Cris took a deep breath, steeling himself for the battle ahead. He was no longer just fighting for Christmas, for the magic of the North Pole—he was fighting for her. For them. And he wasn't going to let Frost take any of that away.

With one last lingering kiss, Cris turned back to the defensive screens. He was determined they would protect the North Pole, defeat Frost, and secure the futures of Christmas and themselves.

∼

Cris watched as Keely paced the command center, her energy palpable as she outlined her plan. The glow of purpose in her eyes was infectious, and despite the ever-present danger, he found himself caught up in her vision.

"We can do this, Cris," she said, her hands moving animatedly as she described the toy she wanted to create. "We've been thinking too small. The toys I've been designing, they're good, but this—this will be revolutionary. It'll do more than spark joy; it will reignite belief. Children all over the world still want to believe in magic, but we need to give them something that brings that feeling back to life."

"She's not wrong, Cris," said Tinker.

Keely paused, her breath quickening with excitement as she continued. "This toy won't just be another gadget. It'll be something that reaches beyond imagination—something that taps into the very essence of what Christmas is about. Joy, wonder, hope. We can build it to interact with kids on a deeper level, using magic to create personalized experiences for each child. We'll light up their hearts, and that belief will strengthen Christmas magic."

"We can do this," agreed Holly.

Cris leaned against the table, arms crossed, listening intently. As much as he admired her passion, there was a flicker of concern deep in his chest. She was right, of course. The plan was brilliant, and if anyone could pull it off, it was Keely and her team.

"And you think this will work?" Cris asked, his voice quiet, though he already knew the answer.

Keely's eyes softened as she approached him, her excitement tempered by a calm certainty. "I know it will. This toy will remind children—and adults—what it feels like to believe. It's what we need. And it's what Christmas needs."

Cris reached out, taking her hand in his. Her skin was warm, her pulse steady beneath his touch, and that simple connection grounded him. "It's risky, Keely. If this doesn't work..."

She met his gaze, her expression steady but filled with emotion. "If it doesn't work, we'll find another way. But we can't just sit here waiting for Frost to make his next move. We need to give the world a reason to believe again."

"Yeah," said Holly, who had become Keely's primary assistant and chief cheerleader. "We need to take the fight to him."

Cris exhaled, squeezing Keely's hand as he pulled her closer. He admired her courage, her willingness to throw herself into this fight without hesitation. She had come here, a stranger to this magical world, and now she was its best chance for survival. And that both thrilled and terrified him.

"I believe in you," Cris murmured, his voice thick with emotion. "I always have."

Her lips curved into a soft smile as she leaned into him, resting her head against his chest. The quiet between them stretched, the weight of the world momentarily lifting as they stood there, connected by something deeper than words.

But even as they shared this quiet moment, the danger lingered on the horizon. Cris knew Frost wouldn't stop until he had drained the last bit of Christmas magic. The North Pole might have won today's battle, but the war was far from over.

Keely shifted against him, pulling back slightly to look up at him. Her hand remained on his chest, her fingers tracing slow, comforting patterns over his heart. "I'm not afraid of the danger," she whispered. "I'm afraid of not doing enough. I want to help. I need to help."

Cris's chest tightened, the depth of her words hitting him hard. She wasn't just talking about the North Pole; she was talking about them, about the connection that had grown between them since the moment they met. The bond that felt as though it had been written in the stars.

"You're already doing more than enough," Cris said, his voice low.

Keely's eyes flickered with emotion, her breath catching as she gazed up at him; Cris felt the world slow around them, the intensity of their connection deepening. He leaned down, capturing her lips in a soft, lingering kiss, his hands sliding to her waist, pulling her closer. The kiss was tender, a shared promise in the midst of chaos. It was a moment just for them, away from the storm that raged around them.

When they finally broke apart, Cris's forehead rested against hers, their breaths mingling in the cold air. "I don't know what's going to happen next," he admitted, his voice barely above a whisper, "but whatever it is, it'll be all right as long as I have you."

Keely smiled, her fingers brushing over his cheek. "Then everything will be all right," she whispered softly.

Holly and Tinker groaned. "Get out," ordered Cris with mock severity.

Later that night, Cris took Keely outside, leading her to a small, quiet clearing beyond the workshop. Above them, the sky shimmered with the breathtaking beauty of the Northern Lights, vibrant streaks of green, purple, and blue dancing across the horizon. It was a sight that had always filled Cris with awe, a reminder of the magic that pulsed through this place, through him.

Keely's eyes widened in wonder as she gazed up at the sky, her breath visible in the cold air. "It's beautiful," she whispered, her voice full of reverence.

Cris smiled, watching her face light up with the same awe he felt. He had seen the Northern Lights countless times, but seeing them with her, through Keely's eyes, made them feel new again, more magical than ever.

"It is," Cris said, his gaze never leaving her. "But not as beautiful as you."

Keely blushed, her eyes darting to his, and for a moment, the intensity between them flared again. There, under the glow of the Northern Lights, Cris felt the weight of his love for her. It wasn't just attraction or chemistry—it was something more. Something timeless.

He reached for her hand, pulling her close as the lights danced above them. "No matter what happens, no matter what Frost does, I'm not letting go of you."

Keely looked up at him, her eyes shining with unshed emotion. "I'm not letting go either, Cris."

Standing beneath the sky painted with magic, Cris knew that whatever happened next—whatever Frost threw at them—they would face it and him and they would defeat him.

As the lights above them shimmered and the cold wrapped around them, Cris pulled Keely closer, kissing her again—slow, deep, full of promise. For now, even with the storm on the horizon, everything was perfect, but tomorrow, the fight for Christmas would begin anew.

CHAPTER
TEN
KEELY

Keely sat hunched over the workbench, her hands moving swiftly as she adjusted the intricate wiring of the toy prototype in front of her. Her fingers ached from hours of tinkering, but she didn't care. Time was running out, and this toy was their best hope to save Christmas. She felt the weight of the responsibility. She was sure that every second she poured into perfecting the design and every ounce of magic the elves were able to infuse into it brought them closer to the breakthrough they needed.

This toy wasn't just some abstract project—it was a testament to everything she had learned since arriving at the North Pole. More than that, it embodied the spirit of joy and wonder that lay at the heart of

Christmas. Those who lived and worked here had opened her eyes to the true meaning behind the magic, and now she was determined to give that same belief back to the world.

Her hands stilled for a moment, and she glanced over her shoulder. Cris stood behind her, watching her work with his arms crossed, his expression both proud and intent. His presence radiated warmth despite the cold air, and the space between them felt charged. There was no hiding the intensity in his gaze, and it wasn't just admiration for her work that filled his eyes.

The tension that had simmered between them since the moment they'd met had grown, building into something undeniable. The way he stood close, the subtle brush of his hand on her back whenever he reached over to help—each touch sparked something deeper.

Keely turned her attention back to the toy, but the awareness of him so near made it impossible to ignore the connection they shared. She adjusted one final piece, her heart racing as she sensed his approach, felt the heat of him drawing closer.

"You're almost there," Cris murmured, his voice low and full of quiet intensity. He placed a hand on her shoulder, his fingers trailing down her arm, sending shivers through her despite the warmth of his touch.

Keely smiled faintly, her breath catching as she leaned back slightly into his touch. "We're almost there. This was a team effort. I never could have done anything without you and everybody else here."

Cris's grip tightened, his hand sliding down to rest on her waist. "What you've done has always been inside you. We just gave you the tools you needed." His voice dropped lower, rough with emotion, and Keely could hear the passion beneath the words, not just for her work, but for her.

She turned, meeting his eyes, and the air between them grew heavy with desire. He didn't wait for her to say more. His lips found hers in a heated kiss, his arms pulling her close, as if he couldn't get enough of her. Keely melted into him, her hands gripping his shirt as the kiss deepened, their connection flaring to life with a heat that had been simmering for days.

Cris's hands slid over her waist, pulling her tighter against him as the world around them faded. It was just them, wrapped in passion and the intensity of their bond, their bodies pressed close, the air between them buzzing with everything they had held back.

When they finally pulled apart, both were breathing heavily, their foreheads resting against each other as they tried to steady themselves. Cris's hand cupped her cheek, his thumb brushing over her skin as if he was memorizing the feel of her.

"We'll finish this," he murmured, his voice rough with emotion.

They stood there for a moment, locked in that quiet, shared space where words weren't needed.

Reluctantly, Keely turned back to the workbench, her fingers flying over the final adjustments. Cris stood beside her, watching her with that same fierce intensity, his presence steady and grounding. She could feel him, every subtle touch and glance reminding her of the connection they now shared.

Finally, with a few more careful twists and adjustments, the toy was complete. Keely stepped back, her heart racing as she stared down at the small, unassuming object in front of her. "It's done," she whispered.

Cris nodded. "It's perfect."

But even as they stood there, a sense of accomplishment washing over them, Keely couldn't shake the lingering worry. This toy represented more than just a clever invention—it was a symbol of hope, of belief. If it didn't work, if it couldn't reignite the magic in children's hearts, then Frost would win, and Christmas would be lost.

Cris seemed to sense her unease, his hand brushing lightly over her back. "No matter what happens, we've done everything we can. And without you we'd never have gotten this far. Hell, I'm not sure we would have survived Frost's first attack."

Keely nodded, though her heart still pounded with

the weight of what was to come. "I just hope it's enough."

As the evening wore on, the final preparations were made for the toy's reveal. The tension of the day had left Keely feeling drained, and when Cris suggested stepping outside for some fresh air, she agreed without hesitation.

They walked through the snow in silence, their footsteps muffled by the soft powder beneath them. Above them, the Northern Lights danced, casting shimmering streaks of green and blue across the sky. Keely paused, her breath catching as she gazed up at the brilliant display.

"It's beautiful," she whispered, awestruck by the sight.

Cris stood beside her, his arm slipping around her waist as he pulled her close. "Not as beautiful as you."

Keely blushed, leaning into him as they stood beneath the lights. The quiet moment was a welcome relief from the chaos and pressure of the day. For the first time in what felt like hours, Keely felt a sense of peace, of calm, as they stood there under the vast sky.

"I'm glad you brought me here," Keely said softly, her voice full of emotion. "I didn't know how much I needed this."

Cris pressed a kiss to her temple, his breath warm against her skin. "I'm glad you're here, too."

The words hung between them, filled with a quiet promise. Keely rested her head against Cris's shoulder. For now, they allowed themselves to savor the peace, knowing the storm was coming.

"We've done all we can do for the night. Let's head home," Cris murmured, his voice rough with need as he took her hand.

She followed him into the warmth and intimacy of what was now their cabin, turning to face him as he closed the door. He reached for her and began to peel away the layers of clothing as she did the same for him. They stood in the soft glow of the firelight, watching each other.

"You're so beautiful," he whispered. "You're everything I didn't know I needed and even more than I ever wanted."

He led her into the bedroom and helped her into bed with reverent hands. A shiver raced up her spine as he kissed her belly before moving lower, parting her thighs with a gentleness that belied his fiery gaze.

"I've been dreaming about this all day. That's wrong, right? We're trying to save Christmas, and I keep thinking about feasting on your pussy," he said with a chuckle.

Cris's hands were a soft whisper against her heated skin, grazing her nipples and sending waves of pleasure coursing through her. A quiet moan escaped her lips as he silenced any doubts she had about the toy or their relationship. Her hands fisted the sheets as he settled in—nuzzling, licking, sucking and nipping at her. The tension within her coiled tighter, each pull of his lips drawing her closer to the edge of ecstasy she now knew to expect with him.

"Cris," she gasped, her voice breaking on his name.

"That's right baby, come for me," he murmured between kisses, his voice rough and raw from his own need.

The world narrowed down to the sensation of his mouth, the mastery of his touch, and the overwhelming certainty that she was about to shatter into thousands of pieces. When the climax hit, it was like a supernova inside her, dazzling and all-consuming. Her back arched off the bed, every muscle tense as wave after wave of ecstasy ripped through her.

Keely cried out, a testament to the amazing revelation he never failed to bring forth from her depths. It left her breathless and clinging to the remnants of earth-shattering bliss.

As the aftershocks of her climax subsided, Cris's movements became a languid crawl up her body, his skin scorching all along hers. Her hands found him, hard and insistent, and she wrapped her fingers around his length. His breath hitched as she began to stroke, a rhythmic pull that matched the still-rapid beating of her heart.

"Cris," she murmured, feeling the raw power of his need pressing into her palm.

The corners of his mouth lifted in a half-smile filled with promise before his lips crushed against hers. The kiss was a maelstrom, devouring any remnants of restraint. Here in this time and in this place, there was only the two of them, the heat of their bodies entwined, and the thundering pulse of desire that demanded fulfillment.

His length pressed at her entrance and with a gentle but firm push, he entered her. The fullness, the intimate connection, sent ripples of pleasure coursing through her.

"Cris..." The word was a sigh and a prayer as she wrapped her legs around his waist, drawing him deeper.

He moved strong and steady within her, each thrust punctuated by a shared breath, a shared heartbeat. They moved in sync, a dance as old as time yet as fresh and new as the first time.

The world outside ceased to exist. Nothing could touch her here, not the shadows of doubts nor the whispers of fear of what might come. In Cris's arms, entwined with his soul, she felt invincible.

He quickened the rhythm, a crescendo of motion and emotion that spiraled tighter with every thrust. The heat of his body seared against hers, an inferno that promised to consume them both. Keely clung to

Cris, her fingers digging into the cords of muscle along his back, each movement driving them both closer to the edge.

"Cris," she gasped, her voice hitching as the building pleasure coiled within her. With every stroke, he hit a depth that sent the lights of the Aurora Borealis bursting behind her closed eyelids.

"That's my good mate," he praised, his breath hot against her ear, his voice a rough whisper that wove through the haze of her senses.

And with those words, the explosion of bliss was blinding, all-consuming. Her body shook with the force of it, waves of ecstasy rolling through her in a relentless cascade. She cried out, a sound that echoed off the walls, raw and full of wonder.

"God, yes... Keely," Cris groaned, his own release following close on the heels of her own. She felt him shudder, his body tensing above her in powerful spasms, and then he collapsed, his weight a comforting pressure that anchored her to the here and now.

Lying beneath him, she held him close, feeling the aftershocks tremble through them both. A profound stillness enveloped the room, their mingled breaths the only sound. His heartbeat pounded against her chest, a drumbeat that matched her own.

In that moment, wrapped in the sanctuary of Cris's arms, she dared to hope, dared to believe.

"Stay with me," he whispered into the quiet, his voice barely there but heavy with desire.

"Always," she answered, her lips sealing the vow.

～

The following day, Cris was up earlier than usual. He wanted to check their defenses and wanted her to sleep. When she woke, she got dressed and headed to the workshop. The elves had been at it all night, and she sent them to their beds to rest. If Cris was right, they were going to need all their energy before the day was through.

Keely felt the chill before she saw him. The temperature in the workshop dropped so suddenly, it was as though the warmth and life had been sucked from the air. Her breath fogged in front of her as she turned, heart pounding, to see Frost stepping through the doorway, his form cutting an imposing figure against the soft glow of the workshop's lights. His eyes gleamed with malevolent intent, cold and sharp like shards of ice.

"Well, well," Frost said with a slow, predatory smile, his voice sending a shiver down Keely's spine. "I see I've come just in time. You've created something very special, haven't you?"

Keely's heart raced as she stepped in front of the workbench, instinctively shielding the miracle toy they'd just finished. She couldn't let Frost get his hands on it. This toy was the key to saving Christmas, the one thing that could restore the magic. And she was pretty damn sure Frost knew it.

"Stay back," Keely warned, her voice stronger than she felt. Her palms were clammy, her pulse thundering in her ears. She had faced Frost's minions before, but this was different. Frost radiated a power that was ancient, dark, and terribly cold.

Frost chuckled, his icy gaze flickering between Keely and the toy. "You're bold, I'll give you that," he said, stepping closer, frost spreading across the floor with each step. "But surely you don't think you can stop me. I've been planning this for centuries. I've drained the magic of countless Christmases. I've stolen the heart of this place right from under their noses. And now..." His gaze darkened. "Now I'll take what you've created."

Panic surged through Keely, but she swallowed it down, forcing herself to think. She wasn't magical like Cris or the elves, but she had something Frost didn't—belief. Belief in the magic of Christmas, in the people here at the North Pole, in the spirit of joy and wonder that had brought her into this world. She just had to find a way to tap into it.

As Frost took another step forward, Keely felt a surge of energy deep inside her. It was faint at first, but as she focused on the feelings—the joy, the love she had found here, and the deep bond she shared with Cris—it began to grow. She wasn't powerless. She had brought her own kind of magic here—her belief.

"You don't understand," Keely said, her voice steady despite the fear gnawing at her insides. "You can't destroy Christmas magic because it doesn't come from a place or a toy. It comes from the people who believe in it. And as long as there are people who believe, you'll never win."

Frost's smile faltered, just for a moment, but the brief flicker of uncertainty was enough to make Keely push harder. She could feel the energy inside her building, a spark of magic she hadn't known existed until now.

"I believe in this place," Keely continued, stepping toward him now, her heart pounding with the force of the magic surging through her. "I believe in Cris, in Santa, in the elves, and everyone else here. Christmas isn't just about presents and toys. It's not about a certain date or even a season—it's about hope, about love, and the magic that connects all of us. That's the real magic. You've never understood that, and you'll never take that away."

As the words left her lips, she could feel it—a powerful surge of pure warmth and energy. It wasn't just belief—it was the very essence of Christmas. The workshop around her seemed to glow with it, the air humming with energy as her conviction turned into something more. Something real. Something magical.

Frost staggered back, his eyes widening as the air around them crackled with power. He raised a hand as if to shield himself, but it was too late. Keely felt the magic rush out of her, a pure burst of energy that filled the workshop, radiating from her like the Northern Lights above. It was blinding, overwhelming, and filled with every ounce of belief and love she held inside her.

The magic slammed into Frost with the force of a super nova—brilliant and blinding. His form seemed to flicker and waver, and he struggled against the onslaught of power, but he couldn't hold on. With a furious snarl, he whirled around, wrapping his long coat around him with a flourish and vanishing through the door into the frost-laden wind, the icy presence he'd brought with him dissipating like snowflakes melting under a warm sun.

As the energy faded, warmth slowly returned to the room, but Keely's legs buckled beneath her. The rush of magic had drained her completely, leaving her dizzy and light-headed. She barely registered the sound of the door slamming open, or the hurried footsteps rushing toward her. Her vision blurred as the world swayed, her body collapsing to the ground.

"Keely!"

Cris's voice was the last thing she heard before everything went black.

~

When Keely awoke, she was wrapped in a warm blanket, her body cocooned in softness. The steady crackle of a fire and the familiar scent of pine filled the air, and for a moment, she didn't know where she was. But then she felt the comforting weight of a strong arm around her, and the warmth of a familiar presence beside her.

Cris.

She blinked her eyes open, finding herself in his arms, his face hovering inches from hers, his expression a mix of worry and relief.

"I really have to quit doing that—the whole fainting dead away," she said.

"Keely," he breathed, his voice thick. "You're okay."

She nodded weakly, her throat dry, but a small smile tugged at her lips. "I did it," she whispered, the memory of the confrontation flooding back. "I found the magic inside me and drove him away."

Cris let out a shaky breath, his hand cupping her cheek gently. "You did more than that. You used magic —real magic—and a lot of it. Everybody felt it."

Keely's body was still weak, but her spirit was

stronger than ever. "I believed," she whispered. "I believed in you, in this place, in all of it. That's where the real magic came from."

Cris's eyes softened, his thumb brushing over her skin. "I'm so proud of you," he murmured.

There was so much between them now, so much more than just the bond of fated mates. What they had was real, powerful, and unbreakable.

But as much as she wanted to lose herself in him and in the warmth of his arms, Keely knew the battle wasn't over. Frost had been driven away for now, but he wasn't gone for good. There was still so much to do, so much at stake.

"We need to finish this," Keely whispered, her voice stronger now as she pushed herself to sit up, her fingers curling into Cris's shirt.

Cris nodded, his expression darkening with determination. "We will. But right now, you need to rest."

Keely shook her head. "Not yet." Her eyes locked with his, her heart racing at the sight of him so close, his presence grounding her, his touch sparking something deeper. "There's no time to waste. We have to stop him before he comes back."

Cris's hand tightened around hers, his lips pressing against her forehead in a lingering kiss that sent warmth flooding through her. "We will," he promised. "But you dealt Frost a harsh blow—not just physically, but mentally and emotionally. He's going to need time to recover. And next time, you won't have to do it alone."

Keely smiled faintly, the love between them palpable. "Never intended to."

As she rested against him, drawing strength from his presence, she knew that in the end Frost would never be able to defeat those at the North Pole. But for now, they had a magical sleigh ride to help Santa prepare for.

CHAPTER
ELEVEN
KEELY

Keely stood at the heart of the workshop, feeling the electric hum of magic in the air as it swirled around her. It had been transformed into a nexus of energy, the very core of Christmas magic flowing like a current through the space. The twinkling lights seemed brighter, the air richer with possibility, as Cris prepared to channel every bit of that magic into the toy she had created—her miracle toy that would reignite belief in Christmas across the world.

Cris stood beside her, his expression focused and intense as he raised his hands, drawing the magic from the very earth beneath their feet. The elves were circled around them, sealing and helping to focus the magic. Keely could feel the power moving through him, vibrating in the air as it built, gathering strength. The energy was unlike anything she had ever felt before—warm, powerful, and pulsing with life. It was the essence of Christmas, the culmination of joy, love, and wonder.

Her breath caught as she watched him, the sight of Cris standing there, his dark eyes burning with concentration, stirring something deep inside her. He was magnificent, powerful, and utterly captivating. Keely could feel her heart expanding with pride and love as she stood at his side, ready to see their creation come to life.

With a final, graceful gesture, Cris focused all the gathered magic into the toy resting on the workbench, his hands steady, his expression intense. Keely held her breath as she watched the energy flow from him, a stream of shimmering light that seemed to pulse with life. It wrapped around the toy like a warm, protective blanket, the air humming with a quiet, electrifying charge. The toy, which had been a simple, static object just moments before, began to shift, its surface glowing softly.

The glow intensified, casting a gentle light over the workbench and the entire room. Keely could feel it—the magic—tangible and alive, as though it were breathing into the toy, giving it not just life, but meaning. It was as though everything they had worked for

—the countless hours of brainstorming, the intricate adjustments, the fusion of her creative spirit and the powerful magic that came from this place—had culminated in this one moment.

The toy shimmered, its surface gleaming with a soft iridescence as the magic infused it fully. Keely's fingers itched to touch it, to feel the warmth radiating from it, but she held back, too entranced to move. She could hardly believe that this creation, this small and seemingly simple object, now held the power to reignite belief in Christmas for millions of children around the world.

The air around them grew warmer, the energy filling the room with a sense of completion, of something magical and profound taking root. The toy, no longer just a collection of parts, now pulsed with its own gentle heartbeat, as though it had become part of something greater. It was alive in a way that defied explanation.

Keely's chest tightened with emotion as she realized it was done. Their miracle toy, the one they had poured their hearts and souls into, was complete. It wasn't just a toy anymore—it was a symbol of hope, a beacon that would carry the magic of Christmas to every child who held one of the toys that it spread its magic to. Santa would keep the toy beside him in the sleigh and it would imbue every single toy that Santa touched with its magic, and each of the toys would be able to spread the gift.

"It's done," Cris said softly, as though he, too, could hardly believe what they had just accomplished.

Glancing around, she saw all of the elves nodding—their eyes locked on the toy, their faces a reflection of relief and hope.

"It's really done," she repeated.

Cris turned to her, a small smile playing on his lips, though his eyes still held the weight of the magic he had just channeled. "It's ready," he said, his voice low but full of emotion. "That's it, everyone. We did it. This is going to change everything."

A cheer went up, and everyone began to celebrate.

"Ho! Ho! Ho!" said a jolly old man in a red velvet suit, trimmed in ermine.

"Santa!" came the collective cry, as the elves rushed to greet him.

As the final preparations were made, the workshop bustling with elves and reindeer shifters, Cris turned to Santa, who had been overseeing the entire process with a watchful eye. It was nearly time for the journey to begin—Santa's Christmas Eve journey to spread joy and cheer to every corner of the world.

Cris stepped forward, his voice steady but filled with an undercurrent of something deeper. "Before we send you off, there's something I'd like to ask of you."

Santa's eyebrows rose, a knowing twinkle in his

eyes as he looked between Cris and Keely. "Oh? And what might that be?"

Cris's gaze softened as he turned toward Keely, his hand still holding hers, his thumb brushing over her skin. The intensity in his eyes made her heart race, the world around them fading as she focused on him and on the connection they shared.

"I want to ask you to bind me and Keely together," Cris said, his voice low but filled with emotion. "As mates. As partners. I've found my fated mate, and I want her by my side."

Keely's breath caught in her throat as her eyes locked on Cris's, the depth of his love hitting her with the force of an avalanche—he wasn't just asking her to stay. He was asking her to be his, forever.

Santa let out a booming laugh, his belly shaking with mirth. "Well, Cris, that's a fine request. But I believe you've forgotten something rather important." His eyes twinkled as he nodded toward Keely. "I believe you should probably ask her first."

Cris's smile turned sheepish, but the intensity in his gaze never wavered. He turned fully toward Keely, his hand tightening around hers as he stepped closer. "Keely," he began, his voice deep and steady, "I love you. I've known from the moment I met you that you were meant for me. You've not only saved Christmas—you've saved me. Will you join me as my mate and my partner, in this life and all the lives to come? Will you share your joy with me?"

Keely's heart raced as tears welled in her eyes, but they were tears of happiness. There was no hesitation, no doubt. She had never felt more certain of anything in her life. This was where she belonged—with Cris here at the North Pole.

"Yes," she whispered, her voice full of emotion. "Yes, I will."

Cris's smile broke wide, his relief and love palpable. He pulled her into his arms, pressing his forehead against hers as they shared a moment of quiet joy, their hearts beating in sync.

Santa stepped forward, holding a ceremonial ribbon of silver and gold, and a candy-cane knife in his other hand. "Well then," Santa said with a grin, "it seems I have a ceremony to perform."

With reverence, Santa made a small cut in Cris's palm, then in Keely's. He took the shimmering ribbon and gently bound their hands together, the silver and gold glowing with magic as it wrapped around their joined palms.

"By the magic of Christmas, by the love and joy in your hearts, and all of us who support you, I bind you as mates," Santa said, his voice booming with authority and warmth. "May your bond be as strong as the magic that fuels this place, and may you bring happiness to all who cross your path."

The magic in the room surged as the ribbon tightened, sealing their bond. Keely felt a rush of warmth flood her body, her heart swelling as the magic wrapped around them both. It was as though they had been woven into the very fabric of the North Pole itself, their love and connection now a part of the magic that made this place so special.

Cris pulled her close, his lips brushing hers in a soft, lingering kiss, sealing the vows they had just spoken. Keely melted into him, her heart full, knowing they had not only bound themselves to each other but to something far bigger than both of them.

As the ceremony concluded, the sleigh bells jingled, and it was time. Santa gave a hearty laugh as he patted his red suit. "I've got quite the delivery to make tonight," he said, winking at them both. "You've created something truly magical."

Cris and Keely smiled as they helped load Santa's sleigh, the miracle toys glowing with the magic they had infused into them. The air was alive with energy, the North Pole buzzing with anticipation as the reindeer lined up, ready to take off into the night sky.

With the sleigh fully loaded, Santa climbed aboard, giving them a final wave. "Merry Christmas to all, and to all a good night!" he called as the sleigh rose into the sky, the reindeer pulling it higher until it disappeared into the night.

With their hands still bound, the magic of

Christmas and the love between them stronger than ever, Cris and Keely turned, walking hand in hand into the sparkling snow. Their future stretched ahead of them—bright, magical, and full of possibility. They would face whatever came as partners and as mates bound by love and the magic of Christmas.

Also by Delta James

Paranormal Suspense

Copper Canyon Shifters

Alpha's Claim

Alpha's Promise

The Grimm Files

Magic Unleashed

Magic Unbound

Magic Unrestrained

Magic Unlimited

Magic Unmasked

Magic Undaunted

Alaskan Tails

His Rescued Mate

His Secret Mate

His Tainted Mate

His Curvy Mate

His Fiery Mate

His Determined Mate

His Brazen Mate

His Reluctant Mate

His Stubborn Mate

His Relentless Mate

His Spellbound Mate

Shadow Sisters

Shadow Spirit

Silent Shadow

Winged Warriors

Phantom Fire

Wild Fire

Dark Fire

Mystic River Shifters (small town shifter)

Defiant Mate

Savage Mate

Reckless Mate

Shameless Mate

Runaway Mate

Stolen Mate

Bah Humbug Mate

Hidden Mate

Unforeseen Mate

Shadow Mate

Otter Cover Shifters (small town shifters/ spinoff Mystic River)

Suspicious Mate

Unexpected Mate

Substitute Mate

Accidental Mate

Feral Mate

Mystic Mate

Elusive Mate

Mysterious Mate

Syndicate Masters

Midwest

Kiss of Luck

Stroke of Fortune

Twist of Fate

Eastern Seaboard

High Stakes

High Roller

High Bet

La Cosa Nostra

Ruthless Honor

Feral Oath

Defiant Vow

Northern Lights

Alliance

Complication

Judgment

Syndicate Masters

The Bargain

The Pact

The Agreement

The Understanding

The Pledge

Looking Glass Multiverse

Shifted Reality

Shifted Existence

Shifted Dimension

Reign of Fire

Dragon Storm

Dragon Roar

Dragon Fury

Masters of Valor (spin off Masters of the Savoy)

Prophecy

Illusion

Deception

Inheritance

Masters of the Savoy

Advance

Negotiation

Submission

Contract

Bound

Release

Ghost Cat Canyon

Determined

Untamed

Bold

Fearless

Strong

Fated Legacy (spin-off Tangled Vines)

Touch of Fate

Touch of Darkness

Touch of Light

Touch of Fire

Touch of Ice

Touch of Destiny

Tangled Vines (spin-off Wayward Mates)

Corked

Uncorked

Decanted

Breathe

Full Bodied

Late Harvest

Mulled Wine

Wayward Mates

In Vino Veritas

Brought to Heel

Marked and Mated

Mastering His Mate

Taking His Mate

Claimed and Mated

Claimed and Mastered

Hunted and Claimed

Captured and Claimed

Wayward Mates Box Set One

Wayward Mates Box Set Two

Alpha Lords

Warlord

Overlord

Wolflord

Fated

Dragonlord

Contemporary Suspense

Club Tales (spinoff novellas Club series)

Tempting Alec

Enticing Kane

Captivating Nash

Club Series

Carriage House (spinoff Club Southside)

Viktor

Club Southside (spinoff Mercenary Masters)

The Scoundrel

The Scavenger

The Rookie

The Sentinel

The Keeper

The Enforcer

The Player

Mercenary Masters

Devil Dog

Alpha Dog

Bull Dog

Top Dog

Big Dog

Sea Dog

Ice Dog

Mystery, She Wrote

Invitation To Murder

Murder Before Dawn

Hook, Line and Mystery

Paint Me A Murder

Deadline To Murder

Relentless Pursuit (Duet)

To Love a Thief

My Fair Thief

Charade

Wild Mustang

Hampton

Mac

Croft

Noah

Thom

Reid

Crooked Creek Ranch

Taming His Cowgirl

Tamed on the Ranch

Co-writes

Masters of the Deep

[Silent Predator](#)

[Fierce Predator](#)

[Savage Predator](#)

[Wicked Predator](#)

[Deadly Predator](#)

About Delta James

Other books by Delta James: https://www.deltajames.com/

Delta James is a USA Today bestselling paranormal and contemporary romantic suspense author, whose goal is to captivate readers with stories about complex, curvy heroines and the dominant alpha males who adore them. For Delta, romance is more than just a love story; it's a journey with challenges and thrills along the way.

After creating a second chapter for herself that was dramatically different than the first, Delta now resides in Florida where she relaxes on warm summer evenings with her loveable pack of basset hounds as they watch the birds, squirrels and lizards. When not crafting fast-paced tales, she enjoys horseback riding, walks on the beach, and white-water rafting.

Her readers mean the world to her, and Delta tries to interact personally to as many messages as she can. If you'd like to chat or discuss books, you can find Delta on Instagram, Facebook, and in her private reader group

Keep up with Delta on Social Media
[Facebook page](#)
[Facebook group](#)
[Instagram](#)
[TikTok](#)
[Bookbub](#)
[Goodreads](#)
[Patreon](#)

[Signup](#) for my newsletter and

Get the good stuff...
Each month Delta shares her writing updates, novel releases, exclusive content and some fun personal stories.
Plus - there's often a giveaway!

Thank you!

Acknowledgments

Thank you to my Patreon supporters.
I couldn't do this without you!

Lori
Carol Chase
Ellen
Tamara Crooks
Suzy Sawkins
Linda Kniffen-Wager
Karen Somerville
Dawn
Karen D'Angelo
Gina Lundeen